I0658060

DESERT ROSE

WONDER HORSE – BOOK FOUR

BY VICTORIA HARDESTY AND NANCY PEREZ

Authors of Action, Adventure and
Suspense with Arabian Horses

PUBLICATION
CONSULTANTS
We Believe In The Power Of Authors

PO Box 221974 Anchorage, Alaska 99522-1974
books@publicationconsultants.com—www.publicationconsultants.com

ISBN: 978-1-59433-847-2
eBook ISBN: 978-1-59433-848-9

Library of Congress Number: 2018967566

Manufactured in the United States of America.

OTHER BOOKS

BY VICTORIA HARDESTY
AND NANCY PEREZ

Prince Ali – Wonder Horse Book One

La Duquesa – Wonder Horse Book Two

Desperado – Wonder Horse Book Three

DEDICATION

With our gratitude, this book is dedicated to our readers who tell us to keep the stories coming that reflect the core values we all strive to follow.

ACKNOWLEDGEMENTS

We are forever in debt to Rebecca Gordon and Sharon Zaragoza for polishing the rough spots for us. With this book we want to acknowledge Mike who is battling serious cancer treatment but still urges Victoria to put writing in the forefront. And thanks to Ray for sharing his Masters of Fine Arts Degree and artistic experience with us. Those muscles come in handy too. Great husbands!

We also owe a debt of gratitude to Melinda Lawrence of Brashear, Texas for her suggestion of Desert Rose the name of the lead character and for the name of one other main character in this book.

CHAPTER | ONE

Pat, Dave, Wayne, and Merle sat around the table playing poker and taking verbal jabs at each other while they planned their next get rich quick scheme. The table was an old folding table with mismatched chairs they found left in the abandoned mobile home in the desert. Dressed in faded blue jeans, plaid shirts, worn cowboy boots and sweat-stained cowboy hats, they looked like something out of an old '50's Western movie. They sounded a lot like it too.

"I heard he won his futurity and brought home $200,000 in one shot," Merle said. "So I don't think $100,000 is too much to ask."

"Are you sure about that?" Dave asked. "You know how people exaggerate prize money to make their horse look better."

"Yeah, but I heard the same thing m'self," Pat said. "He wins about $5,000 a weekend when the competition is good at local events. I don't think a hundred grand is too much to ask. That'll give us each twenty-five grand. I think we should do it."

"All righty then. Guess we should go ahead with the plan," Dave said. "It's 9:00 p.m. now and it'll take us an hour to get there. Maybe we should get on the road!"

Fifteen minutes later the four men were in an old truck towing a beat up horse trailer, heading for the Garcia's Hacienda Rancho on the outskirts of Apple Valley, California. The Apple Valley address was for convenience only. Mr. Garcia purchased a hundred acres of desert land because it was remote. He loved the beauty in the starkness of it. The dirt was a uniform color of gray-brown. The hills behind the ranch were piles of rocks, some large, some smaller. Many of them were streaked dark from minerals leaching out over the millennia when infrequent monsoon rains fell on the desert.

The ranch house was built as a hacienda with overhanging porches to keep direct sun from the windows and provide a bit of shade. The hacienda was large and gracious. The Garcias decorated the front of the home with desert plantings and rusty artifacts of bygone days. The rear covered patio and pool was opulent with Mexican paver tiles covering the floor and the top of the outdoor kitchen area where Mr. Garcia tested his culinary skills on weekends when the family was in residence.

From the back patio a walkway led to the ranch manager's cottage. It was built to look like the hacienda. It was a second home on the property, currently occupied by John and Rhonda Powell. The barn was a short walk from the cottage. It was also built to look like the hacienda. The thick stuccoed walls kept the interior cool in the summer and warm in the winter. Mr. Garcia paved the aisle with Mexican pavers similar to those used on the back patio, but they had a special non-skid finish on them so the horses wouldn't slip. At the moment, only one horse was in the barn. He was Mr. Garcia's prize stallion, Cut It Out, or Cutter as he was affectionately known.

Mike Hartley of Hartley Ranch in Pinon Hills trained Cutter. Cutter was a handsome example of his breed. He was a golden palomino with two white stockings in the rear and a mane and tail of platinum silk. Mr. Garcia called him his "Caballo de Oro" or golden horse.

Mike Hartley showed Cutter for four years for Mr. Garcia. Cutter won every cutting competition he entered. He was the perfect cow horse. He saw, he selected and he held his cow every time, much of the time with his stare alone. All Mike Hartley had to do was point him in the direction of the herd and hold on. Cutter did all the work. He never let a cow get away. Cutter made his selection quickly. He was quick, edgy, athletic, and tough as nails. He got down and dirty and had fun doing it. As a result, four years later he was the top-rated cow horse on the continent.

Cutter was worth a lot, but he held a special place in Mr. Garcia's heart. From the time he first saw him, he and Mr. Garcia were best buddies. Whenever the family came to the hacienda, Mr. Garcia and Cutter went riding. When Mr. Garcia needed to think about something related to his business, he slipped away and came to the ranch. They disappeared for hours at a time. They returned to the ranch sweaty and tired but invigorated and refreshed. Mr. Garcia received many offers to buy his horse, but he refused to part with him. For Mr. Garcia, Cut It Out was his "Caballo de mi Corazon" in his native tongue. In English it meant his "heart horse."

Pat stopped the truck near the walk-in gate to the ranch. The lights were on inside the hacienda. The men knew they were on timers. They'd been here several times to case the place. The lights were out in the barn and the manager's cottage. The only vehicle in the driveway belonged to the manager. They were good to go.

The four men crept through the walk-in gate and walked quietly to the barn. Dave turned on his flashlight so Wayne could see enough to pull the halter and lead rope off the stall

Cutter was in. He opened the door and stepped inside with the horse. He patted the horse's neck and shoulder and pulled the halter on and buckled it. Dave opened the stall door and Wayne walked out of the stall with the horse. Merle gave the horse a piece of apple from his pocket. The men surrounded the horse, walking back to their truck.

The door to the cottage opened. John Powell stepped out on the porch. He'd heard something outside. Rhonda stood in the doorway with the lights inside the cottage backlighting her.

"Who's there?" John yelled from the porch as he squinted into the darkness.

The four men with Cutter froze for a second before whipping the pistols from their waistbands, pointing them directly at the couple. They cocked their guns.

Rhonda's heart stopped. She heard the four metallic clicks as loud as thunder in the still darkness. She froze as did her husband.

"What do you want?" John asked.

Merle shook his head and said, "We want this horse for a little while. Now I guess we have to take you too. If you have them on you, put your weapons and your phones down on that table and march over here right now and nobody gets hurt."

John and Rhonda did as they were told. Dave and Pat pulled the rolls of duct tape they brought from their pockets. They turned the couple around, pulled their arms behind them and taped their wrists together. They spun them back around and taped their mouths with a strip of tape that wrapped around the back of their necks. Merle pushed the muzzle of his gun into John's stomach.

"Now we are going back to our truck. We're going to put the horse inside the trailer. You and your lady will get in the bed of the truck. You will lie down and remain there until we get where we're going. If we see either of you lift your head, it will be blown off. Do you understand? If you do as you are told, we won't harm you or your lady. Do not mess with us! We mean business! Nod your head if you understand," he told John in a low, menacing voice.

John nodded. He couldn't do anything without endangering Rhonda, and he knew it. He passively went along even though his gut burned to take some action. He had no idea who these four men were or what they wanted with his boss's prize stallion. Alone, he might have tried getting away, but not when it could harm Rhonda. He'd have to wait until they got wherever they were going.

John and Rhonda stumbled in the dark as they walked to the truck and trailer outside the gate. They knew this ground well, but the circumstances were nowhere near normal and they couldn't use their arms for balance. Every time they stumbled they felt the muzzle of a handgun shoved into their backs. They walked as carefully as they could.

Two men took the horse to the rear of the trailer and loaded him, tied him, and closed the trailer door. One of the men got into the bed of the truck and helped pull John and Rhonda over the tailgate while another man pushed them up from behind. The second man used a flashlight briefly. Rhonda saw the license plate on the truck. It was a Texas plate with the map of the state in the center. She caught the last four numbers of the plate, 8346, but couldn't read the first three in the short time the flashlight illuminated it. She repeated the four numbers in her head so she wouldn't forget them. She made up a sentence using those numbers to help her remember them. "I eight three times be-four six" kept rolling in her mind. Focusing on that one little detail kept her from losing her mind to fear.

CHAPTER | TWO

John pulled himself over in the truck bed until his body touched his wife's. He knew she was scared out of her mind. Without hands or his voice, the only thing he could do was touch her with his body. He was scared too. They lay still during the drive. Once the truck turned off the highway, John tried to count minutes in his head, so he would have an idea how far off the highway they traveled. He estimated their speed based on how hard the bumps were on their bodies in the truck bed.

The truck slowed down because the road was unpaved and filled with ruts. They had to get the horse back to the mobile home in good condition. The four men didn't particularly care about the two people in the bed of their truck. In the dark, they had to stop several times to make sure they were on the road and hadn't strayed off it. The road wasn't well traveled when they first discovered it, so it was even more difficult in the dark.

The truck finally pulled up next to the old mobile home. The driver left the headlights on so they could see to get the horse in the makeshift corral they'd constructed earlier that day. One of the men dropped a flake of hay on the ground inside the corral and dumped water from a five-gallon jug in a half barrel just inside the fence. The other two nailed rails up to the corral to close it in. There was no gate.

Then three men helped Rhonda and John out of the bed of the truck and up the steps to the front door. One switched on a lantern inside. John and Rhonda were shoved into the living room, tripping over the torn carpet at the doorway. They noticed the three men in the room with them had masks over their faces, and their hats pulled low on their brows. One of them pushed them down a short hallway to the rear bedroom and pushed them into a seated position on the filthy mattress. One of the other men joined him in the bedroom, with his gun trained on John and Rhonda.

"Either of you two gives us any trouble, and he's goin' to shoot you," the first man said as he pulled the tape off John's arms. He pulled a pair of handcuffs from his rear pocket and latched one end onto John's left wrist. He pulled John toward the headboard of the bed and snapped the other end of the handcuffs around the headboard post. He turned his attention to Rhonda and forced her to the other side of the bed where he removed the tape on her arms, He snapped another set of cuffs onto her right arm and attached it to the other side of the headboard. He stood looking at them from the end of the bed.

"If we hear one peep out of either of you, we'll shoot you and dump your bodies down a mineshaft. Nobody will find you for years and years out here. No one can hear you anyways so don't waste your breath. You behave yourselves, and you have a chance. Do you understand?"

With their mouths still taped shut, all John and Rhonda could do was nod their heads. They understood. They were out in the middle of nowhere and nobody would be looking for them anytime soon. If they kept their cool and went along with the thugs, they might survive.

The two men left the bedroom and closed the door. John reached out his hand and grabbed his wife's. He held it fast in his as he swung his body onto the bed. Rhonda matched him and turned her body into his, laying her head on his chest and cried softly. John used his free arm to hold her close to him. They spent their first miserable night together on the filthy mattress in the abandoned mobile home in the middle of nowhere wondering what the dawn would bring.

The four men gathered around the table in the living room swigging down cold drinks and laughing about the experience.

"When're you gonna call in the ransom demand, Merle?" Dave asked.

"Might 's well get it done," Merle announced as he picked up the burner phone from the table. He dialed the Garcia home phone number in San Juan Capistrano and listened as the phone rang four times before being picked up by the answering machine. He followed directions and waited for the beep. Merle pulled out his best West Texas drawl and spoke. "We have your horse. If you ever want to see him alive again, we want $100,000 in cash, in small unmarked bills. We will give you two days to put the ransom together. Call us back on this number, so we know you got the message. Once you've done that, your timer starts ticking. Forty-eight hours later we pick up the money as we tell you or you will get your horse back dead. Your choice. Speak to you soon."

He hung up and dropped the phone back on the table. "All we gotta do is wait for a call!" he said gleefully as he and the other three men began spending their $25,000 in their heads.

Merle picked up the phone and flipped it on briefly to check the amount of charge left on the battery. It was full. That was good since the only way they had to charge it up was to use the charger in the truck. They now had two more mouths to feed so he'd need to drive to the nearest town in the morning for supplies. He'd put it back on the charger then. He turned the phone to standby and dropped it back on the table. They should have a call in the morning. He didn't want to miss it.

Merle, Dave, Wayne, and Pat had no idea the Garcias were not at home, hadn't been for nearly two months, and they were not expected home anytime soon. They were eight thousand miles away.

CHAPTER | THREE

"*Did you hear what is going on?*" Desert Fire asked Pogo, one of the geldings in the pasture with her and her daughter. "*I heard John and Rhonda. They sounded upset. There was some commotion in front of the barn. There were strange voices that sounded mean. I could hear a horse loaded into a trailer. Was that Cutter?*"

"*I heard something but couldn't see much,*" the gelding answered. "*It's pretty dark out here.*"

Desert Rose wandered over to the fence where her mother stood with Pogo. "*What's up? It's the middle of the night. Shouldn't we all be enjoying some sleep or something?*"

Cash and Billy, the other two geldings in the pasture wandered over out of curiosity. "*Anything going on we should know about?*" Cash asked.

Rosie blew air out of her nostrils. "*Mom was talking to Pogo. They heard a commotion in front of the barn. It sounded like Cutter was loaded in a horse trailer. They heard John and Rhonda's voices, and they didn't sound happy. They also heard some strange voices. One of them sounded threatening. The truck and trailer took off. We can't see much, but it's quiet now so we may as well get some sleep.*"

The horses stood quietly in a group for a few minutes. Pogo wandered off followed by Cash and Billy.

"*I'm a little worried, Rosie. This doesn't feel right. Horses don't leave here in the middle of the night.*" Fire whispered under her breath.

"*Mom, you are such a worry-wart. Things will look better to you in the light of day. Let's get some sleep now, okay?* Rosie nuzzled her mom's neck. "*Don't worry over nothing.*"

CHAPTER | FOUR

It took a week after their return from Colorado for life to settle down into the normal routine at Hartley Ranch. Ginny took five girls and her nephew, Brody, to the Arabian Youth National Championship show in New Mexico. Dear friends and fellow equestrians, the Howard family, met them on the road and the group joined a group brought to New Mexico by Chris O'Neal from Colorado. All the competitors had success at the championship show. The group made a spur of the minute decision to go to Colorado for two days afterward. While the young competitors were out enjoying a trail ride in the foothills of the Rocky Mountains, the second largest forest fire in Colorado history blew up behind them.

Several days of sheer panic followed. The young people found themselves trapped in a canyon that protected them from the fire but prevented them from letting anyone know where and how they were. One horse, Desperado, was credited with saving the lives of nine other horses, nine young people, and his elderly owner when they were found safe at last. Once Ginny Hartley and the rest of the California contingent arrived back at Hartley ranch, press from both print and television inundated them. It took about a week for things to finally die down enough to resume their normal activities at the ranch in Pinon Hills.

It was summer, so there was no school and the girls had plenty of time to ride, practice, and trail ride. They didn't talk much about the experience among themselves, but there was a deep and abiding sense of closeness among them and Brody. They had looked death in the face and survived together.

Maryann Wilcox couldn't get used to the fact her "services" were no longer needed at the ranch. She first came to the ranch as a volunteer to work off the cost of horseback riding lessons. Many things had changed over the past several months with the arrival of grandparents she'd never met. Her mother, Rose, now had the money to pay the board bill for La Duquesa and paid Ginny for Maryann's coaching. Maryann still showed up at the ranch ready to work. She didn't mind cleaning water buckets, mucking stalls, cleaning tack and grooming horses for Ginny. She enjoyed spending the time with Brody and working with the ranch horses.

Celeste Carnegie, Maryann's grandmother, spent a lifetime surrounded by wealthy people who never did physical labor. She loved being surrounded by people who thrived on being outdoors doing physical activities. She spent a lot of time with Ginny while she, her husband Charles, and Maryann's mother Rose were in Colorado. They waited together for information about Maryann and her nine companions during the fire. She and Charles found out they had a granddaughter only a few months ago. They discovered what a delightful young lady she was. In Colorado, they were terrified fate would take her from them too soon.

Celeste felt drawn to Hartley Ranch for the peace she found there in the beauty of the outdoors. She was also drawn to Ginny for her strength and courage during the recent crisis. She respected Rose for her ability to find something to do for others while she waited for news about her only child. She saw the two women as steel over marshmallow. They were both tough on the outside and soft on the inside. Celeste enjoyed sitting on Ginny's back patio overlooking the ranch so she could watch Maryann and the others working and enjoy her views of the desert and the mountains that brought such peace to her soul. She brought Maryann to the ranch that day. Charles had some business to take care of, and Rose was busy with paperwork. Maryann's Great Aunt and Uncle, Adele and Roy had doctor visits. That left her to provide transportation, and she loved doing it.

Maryann found Brody on the ranch and cleaned water buckets with him. The horses were fed. Mike Hartley's crew finished mucking stalls. Mike was working a horse in one of the arenas. Ginny took care of paperwork in her office. Maryann checked the tack room and found it all in order. She and Brody were out of work to do.

"Hey, why don't we go for a ride?" she asked him.

"Sure, where did you want to go?" he asked.

"Let's go south today. Maybe we can find that cabin where Mike and Ginny found La Duquesa. I wonder if anyone lives there yet?"

"I think it's just a weekend cabin. I don't know if anyone lives there all the time. We could check it out if you want to," Brody suggested.

Maryann and Brody pulled horses from their stalls, brushed them down and tacked them up for the ride. Maryann pushed bottles of water into a pouch she attached behind her saddle. They walked their horses outside the barn and mounted. They walked to the arena where Mike was working his horse and let him know they were leaving and which direction they were going. Mike confirmed they both had their cell phones on them and waved them off.

"I can't believe we're back to normal after all that happened in Colorado, can you?" Maryann asked him.

"Me neither. That was intense. If it hadn't been for Desperado, I think we might have burned up in that fire."

"Yeah, my tee-shirt got a few holes in it. I saved it as a souvenir. Do you believe how cold it got at night in that canyon? I know rocks are hard, but those rocks poked me to death until the firemen dropped us sleeping bags and tents. But, I swear some of those rocks still tried to get me even through all that," Maryann laughed.

"My clothes smelled so bad when we got back to Chris's ranch Aunt Ginny made me throw them away!" Brody laughed. "I got holes in mine too. Mine smelled like smoke and dirt and sweat. They were yucky!"

"Why don't you tell me about that horse you liked so much. You know, the one you told me about that belonged to one of Uncle Mike's clients," she asked after a while. "You were the only one of us kids who didn't have your own horse. Todd didn't either, but Hilda gave Desperado to him. I thought that was awesome of her."

"Yeah, that was nice of her. Desperado was probably worth a lot of money, but he sure saved our skins. Aunt Ginny told me Hilda gave Desperado to him for his birthday. She says Hilda is going to stay with Chris and Sharon now since her home burned up. Aunt Ginny also told me Hilda gave all her property to Chris and Sharon too. She told them her own kids would sell it off when she passes away, and she didn't want that to happen."

"Wow! I didn't know that. What are Chris and Sharon going to do with it?" Maryann asked.

"I think Chris and Sharon own their twenty acres and there's one property between theirs and Hilda's forty acres. Ginny said they are going to rebuild the barns and fix the turnouts and use it for boarding and for breeding. Hilda also gave Desperado's mother to Chris and Sharon. They are going to breed her and hope to get another horse as good as Desperado," he said.

"Oh, how neat! I love the babies. Maybe we can get to see the baby someday. Wonder if it will be a colt or a filly this time? But, what about that horse you loved so much. Aren't you going to tell me more about her?"

CHAPTER | FIVE

Brody looked away. The reminder was painful for him. "My Bizzy Izzy? Her real name is Desert Rose. Everybody else calls her Rosie. She was the most beautiful chestnut when she shed out her baby coat. She had a perfect blaze that was wide across her forehead above her eyes and tapered down to a narrow stripe that ran down to her nose. She had four white socks. She was beautiful. She had the face of her mother. Her mother was a purebred Arabian like I told you. Her father was that big sorrel stallion of Uncle Mike's. Her body was compact like an Arabian, but she muscled up pretty good like a Quarter Horse," he told her while he stared out toward the mountains.

"She sounds pretty," Maryann said. "What was she like?"

"She was a firecracker! She was always busy with something. That's why I called her "Bizzy Izzy." She would chase the jolly ball all around her paddock. When she wasn't doing that she pushed rocks with her nose. She was like a perpetual motion machine. She never stopped moving until she fell asleep. She would drop in a heap beside her mother for a nap, then hop back up and do it some more. I was much younger too. She would visit with me and suck on my fingers sometimes. That was okay until she grew teeth. After that, I had to let her know to be careful not to bite me. She liked to play with me. I would chase her in the turnout, and she would chase me. We never caught each other but enjoyed the game. She squealed like a little piggy when she was happy. She knew what time I got home from school and was always waiting for me," he was a little sad as he remembered. He turned his face away from Maryann and stared at the mountains.

"How long was she here at the ranch?" Maryann soldiered on, hoping to hear more about her.

"She was born at the ranch because Mr. Garcia was hoping to build his ranch out here nearby. He and his family live in San Juan Capistrano. I think Becky's parents know him and his wife. They have a great big house in a gated section there, but they can't keep horses at home. He was trying to find a large parcel of land out here and build another home and facility for his horses. He finally did," he told her.

"Why did Uncle Mike train her for cutting? She was half Arabian. Don't they ride Arabians in different disciplines?" she asked.

"Oh, you should have been here! She was put in the large turnout one day when she was about nine months old. She ran around and stretched her legs in that for a while. One of the calves got loose from the calf pen. It wandered around and made its way into the turnout with Rosie. She looked at it and watched it for a couple of minutes, then began to work that calf. She refused to let him get away and finally had him pinned in one corner before Uncle Mike intervened. He had to halter her and put her in her stall to make her give that calf enough space for them to put him away," he laughed. "That's when Uncle Mike decided she was a natural born cow horse."

"Wow! That's amazing! Sounds like she decided what job she wanted to do all by herself," Maryann laughed.

"That she did," Brody laughed. "Uncle Mike had the vet check her legs when she was two and a half and got the go-ahead to get her started. They don't start the Arabians until they are three, but the Quarter Horses start at two. She's half of each. I think he was itching to put her on live cows. You know Uncle Mike also trained Mr. Garcia's stallion, Cutter, don't you?"

"No, I don't think I ever saw him. He must have gone before I came to work for Aunt Ginny."

"I know you are in love with Arabians, but you should have seen Cutter," Brody explained. "He was the neatest stallion on the ranch. His full name is Cut It Out! He came in as a late yearling and Uncle Mike did some groundwork with him until he was ready for a rider. He is beautiful. He's a golden palomino with two white rear stockings and a silver-white mane and tail. Once he got on his back, that horse settled right down to his job. It's no wonder Mr. Garcia thinks that horse walks on water. He calls him his "caballo de oro" or his horse of gold if I got the translation right. Uncle Mike put him on cows, and he never looked back. He showed him for Mr. Garcia for several years. He was the top Cutting Horse in the nation before Mr. Garcia retired him," Brody explained.

"How does Mr. Garcia's stallion have anything to do with Desert Rose?" Maryann asked him.

"He doesn't except for how much alike they are when they are working cows," Brody explained. "When she picked out her cow, she was the same way as Cutter. They never let the cow go. I think there is something in their stare besides their body posture. Both horses get down on that cow. They spin, twist, head it off, and pin it where it can't move without ever touching the cow. You need to watch Uncle Mike work in the arena sometime, although you're probably never going to see a horse do it as well as Cutter or Rosie."

"Out of curiosity, what did Rosie's mother do?" Maryann asked.

"Rosie's mother belonged to Mrs. Garcia. She was her personal riding horse. Mrs. Garcia was a lot more timid about riding than her husband, so Aunt Ginny took her time with her and made sure she was well trained, then gave lessons to Mrs. Garcia on her, so she knew as much as the horse did. Aunt Ginny does that. She doesn't want the horse to go home from school smarter than the owner, as she puts it," Brody laughed.

"That makes a lot of sense when you think about it. Why would anyone spend hundreds of dollars training a horse if you don't know which buttons to push and when to push them when you get the horse back home," Maryann laughed.

Brody and Maryann did find the cabin. La Duquesa was reluctant to take the road down to it, and Maryann didn't want to push her. The two of them stopped the horses at the top of the rise and just looked around from there. Someone had cleaned up the trash around the cabin, the windows looked shut up tight with curtains drawn, the porch was swept off, and it looked ready for a weekend get-away. The corral stood empty. She shuddered thinking about the last time she stood inside it. She was relieved when Maryann turned her away from the cabin, and they walked back to the ranch.

La Duquesa lost a much-loved owner in that cabin. It left a hole in her heart that would never completely heal. Then she spent several months of daily torment and nearly died in that corral. It was a place she never wanted to visit again. There were too many memories for her there. Now she was happy.

She was with the girl she was born to be with. She didn't like reminders of sad or ugly things from the past.

"Can I ask you a silly question?" Maryann asked Brody as they walked away from the hilltop on their horses.

"Sure, ask," Brody said while looking down the road for their next turn.

"How come you live with your Aunt and Uncle? Why don't you live with your parents and where are your parents anyway?"

"Oh, you don't know," Brody sighed. "I'll give you the short version. My mother was Aunt Ginny's sister. My mom and dad brought me and my brother and sister to the ranch for Thanksgiving dinner the year I was four. We had a great time. Aunt Ginny and Uncle Mike had all us kids up on horses for rides in the arena before dinner. My sister, I'm told, was a pretty good rider and she loved the horses. My parents couldn't afford them at the time, but they were saving up so they could buy my sister one. Anyway, we were on our way home when a semi-truck crossed over the center line on the highway and hit our car. My parents died then. My sister died too. My brother and I went to the hospital, and my brother died a few hours later. I was the only one left in my family. Aunt Ginny told me my car seat protected me. Aunt Ginny and Uncle Mike took me home when I got out of the hospital. They became my guardians first, then adopted me. I'm legally their son."

"Oh my goodness. I'm so sorry! I didn't know about your family. I shouldn't have asked you," Maryann said feeling foolish for bringing the topic up.

"Don't be sorry. It happened a long time ago. I'm just lucky I had a wonderful family to go to. I think of them as parents most of the time. I still call them Aunt Ginny and Uncle Mike because that was what I called them since forever. We talked about it. They don't mind at all."

"Didn't Aunt Ginny and Uncle Mike have any kids of their own?" Maryann asked.

"Nope. I don't know the details, but they couldn't have any kids. So, they lucked out and got me!" Brody said with a chuckle.

"Yeah, they got a prize, for sure!" Maryann giggled.

CHAPTER | SIX

The four men sat in the living room of the abandoned double-wide mobile home, sitting around the tattered folding table staring at the cell phone. "What are we going to do now?" Wayne whined. "We talked about taking the horse but we never talked about taking hostages with him!"

"I don't think they can identify us. They were scared out of their minds, and it was pitch dark out there," Merle spoke up. "We need to keep them in the dark somehow. We can't let them see us or identify us."

"What do we do about feeding them and getting them to the bathroom and stuff?" asked Pat. "We may have to keep 'em around for a couple of days, and we'd better have a plan. Or, we could just off 'em and put them in an old mine shaft out here. They won't be found for years if we do that. They'll never identify us that way,"

"Hey, I didn't sign up for no killin'," Wayne whined again. "Horse thieving is bad enough, but I don't wanna get tangled up in killin'!"

"Keep your shirt on! Nobody said we was goin' to kill anything. We have to figure out how to handle 'em until we can cut 'em loose and get outa here," Merle said emphatically.

The men woke about dawn the next morning. Pat started a pot of coffee on the propane stove they'd rigged up and cracked a dozen eggs in a chipped mixing bowl. He peeled potatoes and diced them up with onions while he started frying sausages.

The other three men made their way into the kitchen for breakfast and fixed two additional plates for their hostages. Three of the men pulled up their bandanas and pulled their hats low on their brows. Two took plates of food and one pulled out his gun. They walked the food to the back bedroom and set the plates down within reach of Paula and John and left the room, closing the door behind them.

"What time is it?" Pat asked while shoveling eggs and potatoes in his mouth. Merle looked at his watch.

"'Bout time for the call!" he exclaimed. "It's 8:30. Someone should have seen the message on the machine by now."

*****

The following morning, when their breakfast time came and went without John or Rhonda delivering their usual hay, Rosie's mother was concerned. *"When are we going to get our breakfast?"* she wondered.

"They've been late before when they had something else they needed to take care of first. We'll see them pretty soon now," Rosie suggested.

Rosie spent most of that day watching the caretaker's house, waiting for either John or Rhonda to come outside. She saw nothing. She was hungry. She'd never gone without food this long before. Her mother was getting impatient as well. The geldings were grumbling.

"Drink some water. It will fill your belly for now. Be patient. Someone will be along with our feed soon," Rosie suggested to the other four horses.

She saw nothing but dust blowing across the desert from the occasional summertime hot wind gusts. Not one other thing on the property moved, and she heard no sound from the cabin, barn or main house. By late evening she felt a new sensation in her belly. It was empty, and water didn't fill it for long. It was uncomfortable but not painful, but it caused her concern. She hoped to see John or Rhonda soon. She drank more water and finally slept a few hours on her feet, locking three legs at a time at the knee or hock for support. She woke often and exchanged legs to rest one at a time and kept watching the house. Nothing moved.

****

Nobody called the cell phone. Merle drove to the nearest town and spent more of the money the four men pooled together on food and drinks, charging the cell phone during the drive in and back. Nobody called! Nobody called that entire day, or the next one either. By the evening of the third day, the four men were anxious and tired of hiding from their hostages and sharing their meager food supply with them. They were also getting low on hay for the horse. They'd expected to be on their way back to Texas by now with a hundred thousand dollars to spend.

****

Rosie had never gone without food. By the third day, she was feeling faint from lack of food, and she was alarmed. *"Mom, do you think something happened to John and Rhonda. I know they wouldn't go away and leave us here to starve?"* she asked her mother.

"I don't know," her mother said. *"John and Rhonda are not the kind of people who would abandon us. Something must have happened to them. Cutter is gone too. It must have been him getting into the horse trailer that night. I'm afraid you could be right."*

"We need to think positive! Someone will come. Someone will bring us food. We just need to hang in there a little while longer. Let's drink more water," Rosie tried to assure her mother.

The water buckets on the fence were empty. There was a coating of desert dust in the bottom of each one. The only water left for the horses was the large pasture water tank with the automatic filler. One of the geldings in the pasture, probably Cash, played with the float in the tank and broke it off. The automatic filler was no longer working. During the heat of the day, water evaporated from the surface of the tank. The horses drinking more than usual was depleting the water supply even further. The water level was dropping rapidly. Rosie wondered what would become of her and her mother and their companions once the water was gone. She didn't want to watch her mother die. She didn't want to die and have her mother see that. She was very worried but felt it was important to keep their spirits up if she could.

CHAPTER | SEVEN

John and Rhonda spent every day in the filthy bedroom with the door shut and the windows closed tightly. Neither of them could reach a window to open one. The high temperature of the day was oppressive. They lay on the bed and sweated in the stifling heat.

They often talked about the five horses left at the ranch. They knew the Garcia family was out of the country and there was little likelihood of someone stopping by. They hoped their current situation would be solved so they could get back to the ranch and take care of the horses. The longer their captivity lasted, the more deeply they worried about the horses left without any source of food on the ranch in Apple Valley.

They were escorted at gunpoint to the bathroom twice each day. That was their only time out of the bedroom. The bathroom was closed up tightly. Breathing the foul air nearly overpowered them each time they went to it. There was no running water in there so no way to clean themselves up either.

****

Maryann thought about her conversation with Brody. Something about the look on his face when he talked about Desert Rose proved to her he loved that horse and missed her terribly. She remembered him telling her he didn't feel right about asking Aunt Ginny and Uncle Mike for his own horse after all they'd done for him. Now she knew what they'd done. They took him in as their own after his family was killed and even adopted him, so he had parents again. But she thought Aunt Ginny and Uncle Mike would never hesitate to give Brody his own horse if he asked them. She called her friend Becky Howard to talk to her about it. Becky was Brody's friend too.

"Didn't you know about Brody?" Becky asked when Maryann told her about his opening up to her. "I thought you'd know since you live up there. The accident was so awful. I just assumed the locals would have heard about it."

"No I never heard the story, and it happened a long time ago. I asked Brody why he didn't live with his parents out of curiosity. I know that sometimes happens for different reasons," Maryann answered. She went on to relate his story about Desert Rose. "I know he loved that horse. I'd like to see if it is possible to get her back for him. What do you think?"

"Brody would be so much fun as a competitor! I've seen him ride when I visited Aunt Ginny's place. He would have whipped butt at the Nationals if he had his own horse. Yeah, I'd love to help with that. What are you thinking?"

"Brody told me the Garcias own the horse and they live down in San Juan Capistrano. He says Mr. Garcia is a wealthy businessman, so your folks probably know him. We need to talk to him and see if he'd be willing to sell Desert Rose. What do you think? I can talk to Grandpa about raising the money.

After all Brody did while we were stuck in that canyon during the fire, I'm sure Grandpa would help," Maryann explained.

"Yeah, he was the only one that could figure out how to use that satellite phone. If he hadn't we might still be there," Becky said. "I can talk to my dad and see if he would be willing to help with the money too. I think I may know Mr. Garcia's son, Stevie. He volunteers at the Therapeutic Riding Center where I volunteer here in town. I see him there sometimes. He's got the cutest accent. I think Mr. Garcia is part of the local Rotary Club with my dad. Maybe we can get his phone number that way."

"Great idea! Maybe we can call Mr. Garcia first and see if he's even willing to sell Rosie before we start asking for the money. What do you think?"

"My dad has the Rotary Club roster in his office here at the house. I'll see if I can find it and get the Garcia's phone number. I'll call and see if he will talk to me about it and I'll let you know what he says, okay?" Becky asked.

"That would be great!" Maryann said. "Let's keep our fingers crossed. I know Brody would be so happy to have his Rosie back."

Becky did as promised. She found her dad's Rotary Club roster on his desk and copied the phone number for Mr. Estaban Garcia. She tried calling the number for three days at different times of the day and got no answer at all. She was puzzled. When she thought about it, she realized she had not seen Stevie at the stable for a while either. Were they out of town, on vacation, or did something happen to them she'd not heard about? She asked her dad over dinner that night if he knew anything about the Garcias and had he seen Mr. Garcia lately. Her dad scratched his head and had to admit he hadn't seen him around for a while. He promised to check with his Rotary friends and let her know in a couple of days.

Becky called Maryann that night and told her how she'd been unsuccessful in reaching Mr. Garcia. "They may not be in town," she suggested. "My dad is going to check around and let me know. Do you know if you can get the phone number for their Hacienda Rancho out in the desert? Maybe they are there for a vacation."

"I can probably get a phone number from Aunt Ginny's office," Maryann suggested. "I don't want them to know what we're doing so I'll have to wait for an opportunity to sneak into her office in the barn. I know she keeps most of her ranch records there."

"Great. I'll let you know what my dad finds out. Let me know if you can reach anyone by phone up there," Becky said. "This is quite a mystery. People don't generally fall off the face of the planet without telling someone."

CHAPTER | EIGHT

On the fourth morning after stealing Cutter from the Hacienda Rancho, the cell phone had not rung one time. The four men were getting antsy. "What do we do if he doesn't call us?" Wayne whined. "We're stuck with two hostages and a darned horse we can't take back to Texas with us, for heaven's sake. Handling those hostages is a problem. We take a risk they'll see something they can identify every time we feed them or take them to the bathroom. Maybe we shoulda done like Pat suggested and just get rid of them and dump the bodies down an old mine shaft. They're eating us out of house and home, and we're almost broke. We gotta keep gas money, or we can't get back home either."

"I didn't sign up for no killin' so stop talking crud, will ya," Dave yelled at Wayne. "We're not goin' to kill anyone. Maybe we should send him a ransom note in the mail."

Merle looked at the others. "Lay your cash on the table." He pulled his own money, including change, from his pocket and plunked it down on the folding table. The other three men followed his lead. Merle took the money and added it up, including all the change laying there.

Merle looked at the cash laying there and thought for a minute. "We've got enough together to get us through another six days and still have gas money to get us to Prescott, Arizona. If we don't hear something before then, I think we should head for Prescott. They're having a big rodeo there, and between the four of us, we can make a good chunk of money from bronc and bull riding. We always do. That'll get us back home. I'm going to send the ransom demand in the mail today and give it four more days. If we still haven't heard anything from the owner, we have to give up and leave."

Merle sat at the table and printed the ransom note out carefully in plain block letters, stuck it in an envelope, addressed it to Mr. Esteban Garcia at his home address in San Juan Capistrano. He took it to the post office in Ridgecrest, California, the nearest town to the old mobile home they were squatting in. The clerk told him it would take two days to get there.

"What are we going to do with the hostages and the horse?" Pat asked.

"I don't know. Maybe we should just leave them where they are," Merle said. "We could call from Arizona and let someone know to look for them."

"I'm not going just to leave them here to die like that," Dave said in disgust. "I don't want no part of no killin'!"

"Didn't you just hear me say we can call and let someone know where to find them?" Merle shouted. "If we could find this place, I can tell someone else how to find it again after we leave!"

Merle didn't know the last person who took food to the hostages in the bedroom forgot to shut the door when he left the room. John and Rhonda heard the whole conversation. Rhonda began to cry again. She reached her one hand across the bed to John's and held it tightly as she looked into her husband's eyes. This was it! They were going to leave them handcuffed to the bed to starve to death. She never thought her life would end this way. She wanted to raise two children and see them grow up and get married themselves. She wanted to spoil her grandchildren. She didn't want to die in some forsaken old mobile home in the desert. They had to do something.

That's when she felt it. Something scratched the back of her arm. She lifted her arm and saw it. It was a hairpin that fell out of her hair. She remembered tucking her hair up before going to bed the last night at the ranch. Here was something they might be able to use to open the handcuffs if they were lucky. She showed it to John. She had to move her arm and her body a bit for him to use his right hand and pick it up. He smiled at her. It might work.

John and Rhonda struggled the balance of the day to insert the hairpin in the handcuff on his wrist. She had to stretch her right arm to the point of pain and lay nearly on top of John to reach his left handcuff with her left hand. It was awkward. Rhonda began to lose hope again. John had faith they could get that hairpin to work and remove the cuffs. Just what they would do when they were free, he hadn't worked out yet. But he would think of something. All the while they had to keep an ear out for the sound of someone coming and catching them. It was exhausting.

For two full days after Merle mailed the ransom note to San Juan Capistrano, the four men got along pretty well, playing poker in the evenings for a while before turning in. The third and fourth day didn't go so well. The longer the cell phone did not ring, the more agitated they became. The evening of the third night, Merle had to come between two of them before they came to blows over an issue of no consequence.

"Knock it off, you two," he shouted at both of them. "We said we would wait six days and we're only halfway there now. Don't go getting stupid on me. Calm down!"

CHAPTER | NINE

The five horses abandoned at the Hacienda Rancho were getting frantic. Nobody came with feed. They had plenty of shade in the large enclosure. Mr. Garcia had seen to that when he built the place. The water level in the tank was dropping daily at an alarming rate. The horses could survive for a while without food, but without water in the heat of the desert, they would not survive long at all.

"*Mother, I don't feel well. I'm not hungry anymore, but my body aches and I don't want to move, and my ears are ringing*" Rosie told her mother.

"*Rosie, we all feel that same way. I'm just hoping someone will come and find us before it is too late for us.*" Her mother said with sadness. She felt in her heart they had been abandoned. She knew it was just a matter of time and they would start to die in this heat.

"*Mom, we can't give up. What is the best thing for us to do until they come?*" Rosie asked.

"*In this heat, we should probably all stick together and stay in the shade. Moving around is painful and uses more energy. We should conserve what we have,*" her mother explained.

"*Okay, let's do that. Promise me you won't give up!*" Rosie begged.

****

What no one in California knew at the time was that the Garcia's maid asked for and was granted two weeks vacation to visit her mother in Salinas, California. The house was spotless. There had been no one home for weeks, and it didn't look like the Garcias would be home any time soon. She locked up the house and left the morning Cutter was abducted from the Hacienda Rancho in the desert. There was no one home to answer the phone or take a message.

The day the ransom letter was received at the post office, it was put neatly in a box with other mail received that day. It would remain in that box for another 29 days. Mr. Garcia arranged to have his mail shipped to him once a month to his mother-in-law's address in Spain. The last monthly box left the post office by International Priority Mail the day before.

****

The four cowboys sat in the living room of the mobile home playing cards most of the day. They repeated stories they'd told a million times over about that certain horse in the bronc riding event in Wyoming, that certain young lady in Dallas, and that certain bull in Montana from their days on the rodeo circuit. None of them ever made the top. They didn't have the skill or the brains for it. But they did make money just often enough to keep them hoping for that one big pot they'd win so they could have it all, all the money, all the pretty women, all the new trucks, all the big spread ranches. That dream just kept pulling them along. And they never realized how intoxicating it was. This short stopover into criminal behavior was the first on this scale for any of them. They justified it to themselves. "We're just borrowing the horse for a few days." "We'll give him back." "Nobody's going to get hurt." "We just need a little cash for seed money until we hit it big."

In the bedroom, Rhonda and John worked to get her hairpin in the cuff on either of them, working to exhaustion on first one, then the other. They thought they heard a slight click and caught their breath, refusing to move for a few seconds before they realized it was not the sound of the cuff opening. Rhonda was most affected. Tears streamed down her cheeks when she realized they had not unlocked the handcuff after all. John held her with his free arm. "Honey, it's okay. We're going to get these off, I promise you. And we're going to get out of here. Just let's keep on working at it. We'll get there!" He held her as close as he could for a few more minutes and began working with the hairpin again.

****

Maryann thought about her conversation with Becky and found the perfect time to sneak into Aunt Ginny's office in the barn. Brody was working on the far side of the ranch with his Uncle Mike, and Aunt Ginny ran to town on errands. Grandpa dropped her off at the ranch and had to run an errand himself. He was due back within the hour.

Maryann poked through the file folders until she found one with the Garcia name on it. She pulled it from the cabinet and began looking through the papers inside. She found the address and the phone number for the Hacienda Rancho in Apple Valley. She jotted the information down on a scrap of paper and shoved it deep in her pocket. She neatly put the papers back in their folder and replaced the folder in the cabinet. It had only taken her five minutes. She walked out into the barn aisle and directly to La Duquesa's stall. She and Quesa put in a good thirty-minute workout then Maryann bathed her and brushed her down. She put her in her stall and fed her the treats she'd brought from home. Grandpa arrived at Hartley Ranch just as she finished up.

During the ride back home, Maryann asked, "Grandpa, if you had a good friend and knew they wanted something very much, would you help them get it?"

"That depends. Is it legal?" Grandpa laughed.

Maryann smiled at him across the center console in his Jeep. "Yes, of course!"

"How good a friend might this be?" he asked her.

"A very good friend," she answered.

"I'd say, if this is a very good friend and there's something they would like to have that is legal, then it would be okay to help them get it as long as you are not hurting someone else."

"Thanks, Grandpa." Maryann sat thinking about Desert Rose and Brody the rest of the way home. She sort of had permission to work on this project from her grandfather, whose opinion she valued. She felt a little guilty sneaking into Aunt Ginny's office, but she didn't take anything but a little information. And she put everything back right where she found it. She couldn't wait to call the Hacienda Rancho and talk to Mr. Garcia.

She went to her room when they got home and did just that. The phone rang four times and went to an answering machine. She left a detailed message on the machine and waited for someone to call her back. When she didn't get a call that night, she tried the next morning again. She called several times a day for several days with no return phone call from the Hacienda Rancho.

Maryann thought about the mystery. She knew from Brody that Mr. Garcia had taken all his horses home from Hartley Ranch and he loved his Cutter. He wouldn't sell him. Becky got no answer at the Garcia home in San Juan Capistrano. She was getting no answer to the phone in Apple Valley. There should be some other horses in Apple Valley at the Hacienda Rancho. Brody said there were caretakers at the ranch. He knew them because they had worked for his Uncle Mike in the past and Uncle Mike recommended them to Mr. Garcia for his ranch. Someone should be there to answer the phone or return phone calls. She began to worry.

If the Garcias were not around, the caretakers should be there to care for the horses. Something was very wrong. She felt it and it made her feel a little sick. She asked her grandfather to take a walk with her after dinner so she could talk with him about it. She explained the whole thing to him from the beginning. Neither she nor Becky could reach anyone at either the Garcia home or ranch. She had good reason to believe there were horses at the ranch. She had a very bad feeling about this.

"Grandpa, would you please drive me to the Apple Valley ranch tomorrow morning? I have an awful feeling there may be horses there with no one to care for them. I need to see that they are okay. Would you mind?" she pleaded.

"If what you say is all true, I agree it's something we should look into," he told her. "Let's go tack shopping in the morning as far as anyone else is concerned. That way, if all is well at the ranch, we'll come home and not have to say anything about it. There may be an explanation you haven't thought of."

"Thank you, Grandpa," she hugged him and kissed him on the cheek.

CHAPTER | TEN

John finally heard a distinctive click from Rhonda's handcuff. He pried the cuff open. She was free! Tears formed in her eyes again and she rubbed her wrist with the other hand. Then they heard noises coming from the other part of the house. It sounded like someone was walking down the hallway toward the bedroom. She slipped the cuff back on and clipped it together. They didn't want the men to find them trying to escape. The disappointment nearly crushed her.

John did his best to comfort her. "If we did it once, we can do it again. Let's try again when they settle down out there." Rhonda just nodded her head in defeat. "I got it once, and I think I can remember what pressure I applied where. Once we get you free again, I'll tell you how to manipulate the hairpin to get me loose too. You will have two hands to work with. Then we can get the heck out of this dump!" He smiled at her. "It's going to be okay."

Rhonda wondered if they really would be able to get John free. He'd already tried the headboard of the bed. It was a cast iron headboard, and there was no weakness he could find. There was a large finial at the top that prevented the cuff from slipping over the top. The side rails were attached to the headboard below the mattress. They couldn't slip the cuff down to the bottom. The headboard was too heavy for them to lift anyway. They'd never get the cuff off the bottom of the post either.

The problem was the four men didn't "settle down out there" until long after dark. There had been little light in the room at night since they'd gotten there. But the moon was rising to full. For a little while, it shined directly into the bedroom window. The window was filthy, but the light helped the couple as they struggled with the only hairpin they had. John was able to release the handcuff on Rhonda's wrist. He helped her work on his handcuff. About midnight, as far as they could tell, they heard that final victorious click. He was free also!

They heard the floor squeak every time one of the men came into the room. There were some spots in the flooring that squeaked more than others. John paid attention and managed to avoid the noisiest places on the floor as he crept toward the window on the side wall. The window frame was an old aluminum frame and very difficult to move. He struggled for quite a while before finally getting the window open an inch at a time without making noise. He threw one leg over the lower frame and pulled his other leg out the window so he was sitting on the bottom of the window frame. The moonlight helped. There was nothing below the window. He made his leap of faith and pushed himself out, landing squarely on his feet.

The minute he was outside the mobile home, Rhonda pulled herself into a seated position on the bottom of the window frame. John held his arms up toward her and whispered, "Go ahead and jump. I'll catch you." Rhonda jumped. John steadied her to her feet.

"Now what are we going to do?" she asked him.

"There's a small travel trailer hooked to another truck over there," he said pointing to the opposite side of the mobile home. "Must be where they usually stay. Maybe there's something in there we can use or maybe we can find the keys to one of these trucks."

The couple quietly walked to the travel trailer and found it locked. They did find a few full bottles of fresh water in the bed of the truck, which was also locked. They stuffed their pockets with as many bottles of water as they could carry and headed into the desert, giving thanks for a full moon that night. They didn't have much time. It would be first light in a few hours. They needed to be far away from here before then.

CHAPTER | ELEVEN

Maryann was up early the next morning. Her sense of urgency about the horses at Hacienda Rancho grew by the minute. She played with her breakfast, showered and got into her clothes and sat in her room waiting for her grandfather. She didn't want to say anything to her mother in case she was wrong. She was out of her room and down the hall toward the front door the minute she heard her grandfather's Jeep in the driveway.

"Grandpa is taking me shopping," she told her mother. "I need a new girth for Quesa. The one we've been using is getting dirty. The spots aren't coming off. I think I have to retire it for everyday use. I need a new one for show."

Rose kissed her daughter on the forehead. "Okay, but give me a call if you're not going to make it back in time for lunch, will you?"

"Sure, Mom. See you later," Maryann said as she was rushing out the door.

Maryann got into her grandfather's Jeep and showed him the directions she'd printed out the previous evening. The Hacienda Rancho was way out in the desert with nothing around it for a couple of miles. Most of the way was on pavement, but they had to make the last mile or so on a well-maintained dirt road.

Rosie saw the Jeep coming down the dirt road. It was the first vehicle they'd seen on the road since that awful night they were abandoned. She watched, begging the car to stop at this property. If she'd had fingers on her feet, she would have crossed them on all four feet.

As soon as they saw the beautiful fencing along the front of the property and the gracious Spanish style Hacienda, she said, "This has to be it!" Her grandfather pulled up to the closed driveway gate. There was one truck in the driveway. No one seemed to be around on the property, at least not that they could see. Maryann led the way through the walk-in gate and knocked at the front door of the hacienda. There was no answer at the door. She and grandpa walked around the house toward the barn. They saw from a distance that one stall door was open. Maryann noticed the large turnout around behind the barn and walked over toward it.

Rosie watched the girl walking toward the paddock fence. At last! Someone did come! She whinnied as loud as she could, then stood and shook the dust of the desert off her coat. She didn't have the strength to gallop, but she began to trot toward the fence as fast as she was able to.

Maryann was stunned at what she saw. There were five horses in the paddock, two of which were laying on the ground, not moving. The ones on their feet looked awful. Their ribs were showing, and their spines were showing. Their hip bones were showing as well. All of them had their heads hanging except the chestnut mare trotting toward her. The others showed no interest in the visitors.

Grandpa followed Maryann but stopped short when he noticed the door to the caretaker's cottage was standing open.

He saw a shotgun or rifle of some type standing against the door frame outside the cottage. It looked like two cell phones were sitting on the table on the patio in front of the cottage as well. Lights were on inside the cottage. His red flag went up when he thought about those items, the open stall door in the barn and the single vehicle sitting in the driveway.

"Maryann, we need to call the sheriff. I think something is wrong here," Grandpa said to her.

"Grandpa, there's absolutely something wrong here. Look at the horses! They look like they are dying. They need help bad, and they need it now. Can we call Uncle Mike and Aunt Ginny?"

"Yes, you call Mike and Ginny now and have them bring a horse trailer. I'm going to call the sheriff's office. Don't touch anything except the water hose and the hay. You'd better get those poor horses something to eat."

Maryann called Hartley Ranch and reached Aunt Ginny. In a rush, she explained what was going on at the Hacienda Rancho. "Please Aunt Ginny, can you and Uncle Mike bring your large horse trailer here as soon as possible. There are five horses here in really bad shape. I don't know how long they've gone without food. I haven't checked their water yet but I will the minute I hang up the phone. We're waiting for the sheriff to show up here too. Something bad happened here. We've got to save these horses!"

Ginny ran out back to the paddock where Mike was working one of his reiners. She yelled at him. He rode over to the fence. She explained the call from Maryann. Mike climbed off his horse and handed the horse to one of his guys to put away. He rushed to get their large horse trailer hooked to their truck. Ginny jumped into the passenger side. They were off in a cloud of dust heading for Apple Valley as quickly as possible.

Mike and Ginny arrived at the Hacienda Rancho minutes before the sheriff arrived. Ginny went with Maryann to the large paddock to see the horses in question. She was sickened by what she saw. The horses all needed help quickly. In the heat, they had gone without food for more than a week at least by her estimate, and they were all showing signs of starvation. Ginny suggested Maryann give each horse a quarter of a flake of hay for now. She pulled out her cell phone and talked to her vet. He would meet them at Hartley Ranch within two and a half hours. She helped Maryann fill water buckets with fresh water which the five horses drank eagerly. The two who were laying down when Maryann arrived got to their feet and slowly walked to the fence for fresh water. Maryann carefully doled out the hay as Ginny suggested while Ginny climbed over the rail and began checking each horse over gently. The only thing she found on any of them were rub marks where they'd rubbed the hair off hocks and hip bone areas because they'd been laying down a lot in the past several days.

Mike and Grandpa talked with the deputy sheriff when he arrived. They showed him what caused their concern, the open door of the caretaker's cottage, the shotgun leaning against the door on the outside, the cell phones and the truck in the driveway. Mike explained, "I know John and Rhonda very well. They worked for me. They are excellent horsemen and extremely reliable people. I was the one who recommended them for the caretaker position here. The owner is Esteban Garcia, a client, and a friend of ours. The one thing I need to bring up is one horse is missing. The horse that should have been in that open barn stall is Mr. Garcia's prize stallion. That horse is worth a half a million dollars at least."

The deputy sheriff's eyebrows raised at that comment. "Maybe that's what happened here. Maybe somebody came in to steal the horse, and the caretakers got in the way. You didn't see any signs of a struggle when you got here did you?"

Grandpa Carnegie looked at him, "We didn't see any blood if that's what you mean. If we'd seen that, we would never have come on the property. We'd have called you first. We didn't notice anything at first. The walk-in gate was closed. We came in through that and knocked at the main house. When we didn't get an answer, we came around back here looking for anyone on the property. We didn't see anyone. My granddaughter did see that the horses out back are not in good shape. They look starved like they've been without food for some time. That's when I noticed the open door, the gun, and cell phones and decided it was best to call you."

"Did you enter the cottage or touch the gun or the phones?" the deputy asked.

"No, as soon as I put two and two together, we stayed away so we wouldn't contaminate anything for you and your people," Grandpa Carnegie said. "Can we ask for your permission to remove the remaining five horses and get them the help they need?"

"I need to call this in first. We should get a crime scene investigator out here. I'll ask my watch commander about the horses. We don't have facilities to take them to. If you two will give me your information, I can pass it on and suggest you are probably the best place for them right now. Mike, I know you by reputation, and my daughter has been bugging me to let her take lessons from your wife. We'll be seeing you at your ranch soon anyway."

The deputy walked back to his patrol car and called his watch commander. He talked for a few minutes then walked back to where Mike and Grandpa Carnegie were waiting. He jotted down their names, phone numbers, and addresses for his records. "My watch commander said you could take the horses back to your ranch. Here's my card. Please let me know how they do and if you can get an estimate of how long they've been without food from your vet. It will help us figure out when the caretakers disappeared from here," he told the men. "I've got to wait here. He's sending out some people to go over the crime scene. Thank goodness I don't think there's been a murder here. With the door open in this heat, we'd have known that right away from the smell."

Mike, Ginny, Maryann, and Grandpa began walking the horses out to the trailer for the ride to Hartley Ranch. Maryann recognized Rosie immediately from Brody's description – Chestnut, beautiful blaze wide above the eyes tapering to the nose and four white socks. She was the first horse at the fence when they got there. Maryann walked her to the trailer herself and talked to her as they walked, "Rosie, you're going to be okay. We're taking you back to the ranch where you were born so we can help you." Desert Rose was numb with relief. Her blind faith had worked. Someone did come for them! She knew Uncle Mike and Aunt Ginny. She was going to be okay, and so were the others, including her mother. She didn't want to admit she was on the verge of truly giving up when Maryann and her grandfather arrived. Would her Brody be there when they got back to the ranch? Would he remember her? She was anxious to find out.

CHAPTER | TWELVE

John led Rhonda away from the mobile home for about a quarter of a mile before he felt it would be safe for them to talk louder than a whisper. He took stock of their situation as they walked. Rhonda had been a vet tech for a small animal hospital a few years ago. She liked the scrubs they wore to work and kept them. She usually wore them to bed at night. This night she was wearing a pair of light cotton scrub pants with a drawstring waist. She'd filled the pockets with water bottles from the truck bed at the camp and tightened the string at her waist so the pants didn't pull off. Her top was a light cotton short-sleeved pullover covered with adorable little animals. It had pockets too that she stuffed with water bottles. She had a pair of thin rubber-soled slippers on her feet. He wore his usual cotton pajama bottoms. He pulled on a cotton tee shirt before opening the door that night. He also stuffed his pockets with water bottles, and he'd tightened the drawstring on his pajama bottoms to keep them up. He wore soft-soled moccasin-style slippers.

The clothes they wore would give them almost no protection from anything. They were light, and that helped in the relative cool of the evening. Their feet were little better than bare. They carried as much water as they could. They had no weapon, no food, and no way to protect themselves from the heat of the sun tomorrow. He picked up a long stick he found hoping it would be enough to scare off any critter that decided they might make a meal or a tasty snack. He realized they would have to find their way to a town or a road or highway before the next day was full on them. He hoped to find a highway with some traffic on it. He fervently hoped they could flag down a traveler on the highway that would take them to the nearest town. He'd never hitch-hiked in his life but had passed by many of them before. Could he get someone to stop for them? Maybe someone would take pity on them because his wife was with him and he wasn't just a single male on the road.

He stood on a small rise in the ground and peered into the darkness in all directions. He hoped to see a slight glimmer of light close to the ground that could give away the location of a town with streetlights on during the night hours. He listened in the still night hoping to hear the sound of wheels on pavement. He was disappointed. He neither saw a glow at the horizon nor heard anything but the whisper of a breeze through the low desert scrub and the yips of a coyote family. He picked a direction and held his wife's hand as they began walking.

Before long they came to another rise in the ground. John talked to Rhonda about making herself as small as possible and creeping as low to the ground as she could. "If they find us missing, they will probably start looking for us. We need to stay low in the high spots so we don't make a perfect profile for them to find."

He and Rhonda squatted close to the ground and nearly crawled over the rise. They didn't stand up again until they were below the highest spot. Rhonda tore the knee of her scrub pants on a rock when she stumbled. She didn't feel blood. She did her best to ignore the stinging of her knee.

John stubbed his toe on a loose rock he didn't see. It tore a small hole in his slipper. "We're going to have to be more careful. Thankfully, we have a full moon out tonight. Let's take it slow and look before we take another step. We can't afford to get hurt out here. We have nothing to use for bleeding. Heaven forbid we break anything," he said to his wife. He was more worried than he let on. If either of them was injured out in the desert, there was no reason to believe someone would find them anytime soon. They had water, but that wouldn't last. They had no food. They had no protection from the sun. They didn't know where they were. He continued to encourage Rhonda. "Take it slow and easy, honey. We'll get there," he said.

John and Rhonda struggled on for the better part of two hours before coming to another decent rise in the landscape. "I think we are far enough away from the camp now. Let's get to the top of that rise and see what we can see or hear. Remember, we're looking for a soft glow along the horizon that might indicate the lights of a town. Either that or maybe we can listen and hear some traffic noise on a paved road, okay?"

Rhonda was more tired than she'd ever been in her life. She was not just tired from wandering around in the desert for several hours, but the stress of being a hostage and the stress of not eating properly and the stress of the heat in the room they were held in all mounted up into fatigue she'd never experienced before.

"Why don't we find a place where I can stop and wait. You go ahead. I have water with me. Come back and get me when you find us help," Rhonda finally said to John.

"Absolutely not!" he told her. "I'm not leaving you. We stick together until we find civilization again, okay."

John puzzled their situation out in his head. When they left the ranch, he was certain they traveled toward the west. When they reached the highway, the truck turned right onto the highway. That would be to the north if his first assumption was correct. When the truck turned off the highway toward the mobile home, the truck turned right again. That would put them traveling to the east. He'd been on a highway a couple of times before that went north from their original location. The desert along that highway had towns alongside, but they were many miles apart. Some seemed abandoned. He recalled there were areas out in the desert favored by dirt bike riders. There were a few main roads off the highway used by the dirt bike people who hauled their campers and trailers out into the desert for weekends. He began to look for signs of dirt bike paths as they continued walking in what he hoped was a southwesterly direction. They would have to find one of those main roads and follow it to the highway.

He put his arm around his wife's shoulder and squeezed it. "We're going to find a road soon. I just know it," he whispered in her ear.

They walked for another three hours under the light of the full moon. John was excited when he began to see signs of dirt bike paths. He didn't want to follow them because he knew they could go in any direction. He had to stay on his path if they were ever going to find a road.

When John turned and saw a slight rosy glow on the horizon behind them, he knew for sure they were walking to the west. The sun rises in the east and sets in the west. He knew the sun's rising would create new problems for them. They were more visible for one thing and the sun's intense heat could cause devastating effects. They had to find help soon and get to shelter. For as far as he could see, there was nothing that would give them shade and protection from the sun. They kept on walking.

"Do you see that?" he asked Rhonda with hope in his voice. "That looks like a real road."

"I think you may be right," she said. "It's bare dirt, but it's wide enough to be a road."

Newly energized by the sight of the road, they increased their speed until they reached it. It was indeed one of the main dirt bike roads into the desert. Weekends were busy with bikers coming in with trucks hauling their campers and travel trailers out into the desert. They walked through one of the campsites. The rock fire-ring protecting the long extinguished campfire was clear enough. They saw tire tracks from trucks and bikes covering the ground. Heavy bootprints showed where they'd made camp and relaxed in the evenings after a day of tearing up the desert.

John studied the truck and trailer tire prints. The ones leaving the campsite, the ones not driven over, all pointed in the same direction. He and Rhonda walked in that direction, to the west. They traveled several miles before they saw anything moving. It was a car driving north on the highway. John picked his wife up and spun her around, lifting her completely off the ground. "We've found it! We found the road out of here! All we have to do is flag someone down."

Rhonda had tears in her eyes again at the sight of that single little blue car. It represented hope to her.

CHAPTER | THIRTEEN

As soon as the deputy permitted them to take the horses back to Hartley Ranch for rehabilitation, Ginny and Mike started loading them in their trailer with the help of Maryann and Charles Carnegie. Once the last one was in and tied and the rear trailer door secured, Mike and Ginny jumped into their truck for the trip home. Charles and Maryann followed them back to the ranch.

"I've got to get ahold of Esteban Garcia," Mike said. "I've got to find out what he knows about this."

"You're right," Ginny said. "I can handle the horses with Brody, Maryann, and Charles while you try to reach him. I want to be there when Doc Martin shows up. I want him to see the horses to be sure we're covering all the right bases."

The couple sat quietly in the truck for the next several minutes, "You know, I'd like to talk to you about something," Ginny said.

"Go ahead," Mike answered her, glancing at her profile for a second before turning his eyes back on the road.

"I had a conversation with Maryann at the ranch before the deputy showed up and while he was talking to you and

Charles. She told me some pretty interesting things. That young lady has an unusual "spidy-sense" of some kind. She told me that she and Becky Howard had been trying to reach Mr. Garcia for over a week with no luck. She got a bad feeling about the horses she's never even seen before. She talked her grandpa into driving all the way to the ranch this morning to check on them. And, thank goodness she did! Look at what we found. If she hadn't shown up, those horses would have died within a day or two from the looks of them."

"That is pretty weird," Mike acknowledged. "Did she tell you why she and Becky were trying to reach Mr. Garcia?"

"Yes, she did. You know she's a good friend of our Brody. He thinks a lot of her too, by the way. She'd talked to him about why he didn't have a horse of his own. Apparently, he fell in love with that little chestnut mare we have in the back, Rosie. He told Maryann he loved that filly when she was born and loved her as she grew up. It broke his heart when she left one day while he was at school. He's never looked at another horse like that since."

"Are you kidding me?" Mike asked crinkling his brow. "Brody never said one word to me about that filly. I didn't know he was especially attached to her."

"I didn't either," Ginny admitted. "We could easily have talked Mr. Garcia into selling her to us before he took her home. I know he likes her, but his heart was always with Cutter."

"Is that why Becky and Maryann were calling Mr. Garcia? Were they trying to buy the horse for him?"

"Exactly!" Ginny said. "Maryann told me when neither she or Becky could reach Mr. Garcia at his home in San Juan Capistrano or at the Hacienda Rancho, she got worried and had a feeling there was something terribly wrong having to do with six horses. She would have no way of knowing how many horses Mr. Garcia had at the time. But that's why she came out this morning."

Mike had a puzzled look on his face. He stared straight ahead at the road, but the wheels inside his head were spinning like crazy. "Do you think she has a special sense for these things?"

"You mean like extrasensory perception? I call it her "spidy-sense". I don't know, but this is not the first time something unusual has come up in her case. Do you remember me telling you about the first time she rode La Duquesa?"

Mike shook his head but kept his eyes on the road ahead.

"I saw an essay she'd written for school. A teacher friend of mine showed it to me. It told about how she rode a silver mare bareback in the moonlight in her dreams. That's how I happened to bring her on to work off riding lessons in the first place. That essay she wrote included a drawing she'd done of herself riding the mare. The first time she rode Quesa, she did some strange things. She removed the horse's bridle and saddle, then her shoes before she hopped on the horse. She started out riding at the walk and the trot. Then at the canter, she assumed the exact position she'd drawn in that picture. The sun was going down so I saw this in the sunset, but I have to tell you I got chills down my spine looking at her. She and the horse were an exact copy of her drawing, right down to the plaid shirt she wore and the little "L" shaped tear on the left knee of her jeans. I still have that drawing in my office. I'll show it to you."

"Why didn't you tell me about this before?" Mike questioned her.

"Honestly, I didn't believe it myself at the time. But it was enough that I felt drawn to helping her, and that's when I wrote to her grandparents and told them about her. Now, I'm beginning to believe there's more to this than I originally thought. I think when Maryann's little "spidy-senses" go off, I want to know about it right away!" Ginny laughed.

Mike chuckled. "I think you're right. You let me know if that ever happens again. I'd like to know too."

CHAPTER | FOURTEEN

Mike pulled the truck and trailer down in front of the main barn when they got back to the ranch. Charles Carnegie parked in the parking area and came to the barn with Maryann to help unload the horses and put them in stalls. Brody came to join them. Mike pulled the first gelding out. Brody took the lead rope from him and led the horse to a stall. Ginny pulled the second horse out and handed him off to Maryann to put away. Mike pulled the third horse out of the trailer. It happened to be Rosie. She turned her head and spotted Brody coming out of the barn stall. She squealed, lept backward and pulled the lead rope clean out of Mike's hand. She spun for the barn and charged at Brody squealing like a baby horse. She put on the brakes in front of him and pushed her nose in his chest, making little squeaky noises and nickers of sheer happiness. Brody threw his arms around her neck and pushed his face into her skin. Even with his eyes closed, the smile on his face would have lit up the moon in broad daylight.

Mike, Ginny, and Charles Carnegie stood watching the boy and the horse with their mouths open. None of them expected this scene. Maryann stood to one side of the barn laughing out loud.

"Guess she's happy to see you," Maryann told Brody.

"Yeah, I guess she is. I'm happy to see her too. I missed her," Brody finally answered, stepped back and picked up the end of her lead rope. He stood and scratched her withers and talked under his breath to her. She calmed right down. "Come on Izzy, let's get you in a stall so I can go find you some goodies, shall we?" he told her. They walked to the next open stall and walked in side by side. He scratched her itchy places and removed the halter before backing out of the stall and closed the door. Rosie became agitated and screamed out for him, throwing herself from side to side along the front wall of the barn in a panic. Her eyes never left him.

Brody walked back to the front of the stall and began talking to her in a low and soothing tone. "Hey, you don't want to get upset and make all this fuss. I'm just going to find you some goodies. You be a good girl now and wait for me. I'll be right back, I promise!"

Rosie calmed right down and noodled in the feeder for a little grain left there by the previous occupant. Brody walked into the feed room and found a couple of horse cookies and took them back to Rosie. She ate them from his hand, smacking her lips and licking his palms while she squealed with delight.

Mike and Ginny looked at each other incredulously. "Did you know anything about this?" Mike finally asked her.

"No! The first clue I got was what Maryann told me at the ranch before we loaded the horses up," Ginny admitted. "I had no idea these two were so close."

"Let's get the other two out of the trailer so I can get it put away. Then I have to call Esteban Garcia and let him know what's going on here." Mike walked back inside the trailer and unhooked Rosie's mother. He handed her off to Maryann. He unhooked the last horse and walked it out to Ginny, closed the trailer, jumped in the truck and drove to the parking area.

As soon as Mike unhooked the trailer from his truck, he parked the truck, asked one of his guys to clean out the trailer and returned to the barn office. He dug in the files and found Esteban Garcia's cell phone number and dialed it. He listened until the voice mail announcement came on and left him a message. "Esteban, this is Mike Hartley. I need to speak with you urgently. Please call me back at the ranch when you get this message no matter what time. It has to do with your ranch in Apple Valley and your horses. Thank you."

He came out of the office and found Ginny. "You know, if there was no answer at home in San Juan Capistrano and no answer at the Hacienda, they could be in Spain. The family does go there often because they have relatives there. I remember him telling me his wife's parents live there. If so, with the time difference it's in the middle of the night there. I'll give it a few hours before I try calling again."

Ginny was getting small amounts of fresh hay and soaked pellets to the five new horses in the barn while she waited for Doc Martin to arrive. She went into the stalls and checked every horse over before he got there. She noted hock sores, sores on front knees and fetlocks and hip bones from laying on the hard desert soil. The scrapes happened when the horses moved around while getting back on their feet. Ribs, spines and hip bones were protruding on each horse, but she'd seen much worse in the past. She knew decent food, added slowly, would bring them around in a few weeks. She just wanted Doc Martin's opinion in case there was something she'd missed in her examinations.

Doc Martin arrived, looked the horses over and agreed with Ginny's evaluation. He pulled blood from each of them and told her he'd get back to her if he found anything there he didn't expect. He reviewed her feed schedule for the horses and agreed with that as well. Since the horses were owned by a friend of the Hartley's and they were very sure the horses were up to date with their vaccinations, Doc left to see a patient with an emergency within a few minutes.

Ginny was walking out of the barn when the phone rang in her office. She picked up the phone and listened. "Oh, Esteban, I'm so glad to hear from you. Let me get Mike for you."

She went to the barn door and called out to Mike. He hurried back to her office and picked up the phone.

"Hello, Estaban. Good to hear back from you so soon. Where are you now?" Mike said, then listened intently. "Must be the middle of the night for you then," Mike answered. "I've got something to tell you," he said and filled Esteban Garcia in with as much as he knew. He gave him the deputy's name and contact phone number off the card the deputy gave him at the ranch. "Okay, I'll talk to you in a few minutes then," Mike said and hung up the phone.

"They are in Spain. Louisa's mother is ill. They were called over there a month and a half ago," Mike told Ginny. "Esteban is making travel arrangements right now. He's coming home. He's pretty upset about this. He knows Cutter is missing along with John and Rhonda. I told him I'd wait for his call. It's going to take him at least 24 hours to get home with customs, driving time and the long overseas flight. I'll wait here and see if there's anything we can do on this end to help," he explained to his wife. "If Cutter were mine, I'd be doing the same thing."

CHAPTER | FIFTEEN

Wayne and Dave drew the short straws and were the ones who had to give the hostages their bathroom break while Pat fixed breakfast. They walked down the hallway to the master bedroom with their bandanas up over their noses and their hats pulled low on their brows as usual. Dave had his gun out because Wayne needed both hands to open the handcuffs. Wayne threw the door open and stepped inside and halted. Dave nearly ran him over. "Look! They're gone!" Wayne shouted.

"Wadda ya mean they're gone?" Dave shouted back at him.

"Look around dummy," Wayne's voice cracked. "The window is open, the bed is empty, and the handcuffs are hanging from the headboard posts. The hostages are not here! That's what I mean. They are gone!"

The commotion in the bedroom attracted the other two men. Merle came stomping down the hallway with Pat right behind him.

"What's going on in here?" demanded Merle.

"The hostages are gone, Merle. This is what we found when we opened the bedroom door just now," explained Wayne.

"They managed to unlock the handcuffs, open the bedroom window, and they are in the wind by now."

Merle looked around the room in a second. They were gone. How long had they been gone? How far could they have gotten? "Let's go see if we can see them. Each of us takes a different direction. Let's go now!"

The four men rushed out of the mobile home and headed in different directions. They each looked for a hundred yards or so. "They went this way," shouted Pat from the truck and travel trailer. "They took water with them." He followed what tracks he could find for a way and still did not see any signs of life. "They are long gone by now!" he shouted to the others.

The men gathered at the steps of the mobile home. "What are we gonna do now?" asked Pat. He thought maybe they should have just shot them and dumped their bodies down a mine shaft after all. The hostages had been a real pain since they stole the horse.

Merle thought hard. "We don't want to get caught out here. I don't know if they can find this place or bring anyone to it. They've been wandering in the desert for who knows how long. Maybe they'll die out there. But, maybe they won't. We need to make a Plan B now."

"I say we get the heck out of here," Wayne whined. "I didn't sign up for no hostages. We just borrowed us a horse for a couple of days for some quick money. That's not exactly worked out for us now, has it?"

Dave agreed with Wayne. "If we leave now, we can't be convicted of killin'. Let's cut our losses and get out of here. Maybe we should head for that rodeo you were talkin' about. We can always make a few bucks there on broncs and bulls, then head for home."

"What are we goin' to do with that danged horse? We can't take him with us. We got no papers on him, no health certificate or nothing. We can't cross state lines with him. And we can't take him back where we got him so what are we supposed to do with him now?" Pat asked.

"We pack our gear and leave now," Merle said. "Give the horse the food and water we have and leave him. If he lives, he lives. If he dies, he dies. But it won't be on our heads either way. Let's get our stuff together and get out of here. Let's go to Prescott and the next rodeo."

It took them about an hour to get their things packed in the travel trailer, horse trailer, and the trucks. They turned on the highway and drove south to the interchange where they switched directions and headed for Arizona. None of them had much to say on the long drive to Prescott. None of them saw the haggard looking couple in sleeping clothes walking down the dirt road toward the highway when they passed them.

CHAPTER | SIXTEEN

Esteban Garcia got on the phone with his travel agent in California. They were still open. He remembered it was the dead of night for him but business in California was still working. He told the owner what he needed and held on the line as the woman checked flights and seat availability. He was in luck. There was a flight from Madrid to Los Angeles in five hours, and she could get him a seat on that flight. He booked it. He had a few things to do where he was. He talked to Louisa. She agreed he needed to go home and suggested he take their son Stevie with him.

He called his travel agent back and got an additional seat for his son. He would take Stevie home so he could catch up on some of his school stuff. Because of the emergency nature of their trip to Spain, he'd been doing his regular school work by email with his teacher in San Juan Capistrano. He needed to be home for the tests he should be taking to stay current.

He called Louisa's sister who lived an hour away from their parents home. She agreed to come to help Louisa so Esteban and Stevie could go home.

That barely left time for packing Esteban and Stevie for the trip. Esteban tossed the bags in the rental car and drove two hours to the airport in Madrid. He dropped off the car at the rental lot and took the shuttle to the terminal and checked in for their flight. They checked their baggage and walked to the customs area for screening. That took an extra two hours before flight time. They hurried to their departure gate with barely enough time to board the flight. The flight was nonstop to Los Angeles and felt like forever. They had first class seats which were roomier, but it was still tiring to sit for hours in one position. Stevie was able to sleep a good part of the way and watched movies the rest of the time. Estaban could not. He brought his laptop and did some business work. He worried about Cutter and what may have happened at the ranch. He worried about John and Rhonda. From what Mike Hartley told him, their vehicle was still in the driveway and they left their phones on the patio table in front of their home. It seemed unlikely they left willingly.

He spent a good deal of the time daydreaming. He remembered buying Cut It Out as a youngster. He was struck by the beauty of the horse. The horse's coat shimmered like gold in the sunlight and his mane and tail like silver. He was one handsome individual. He was always attracted to palomino horses, but he had a chance to own this one. Cutter had a certain dignity about him, but he was also very playful at times. They became great buddies. Esteban had a wonderful recommendation to Mike Hartley as a trainer for his new colt. He drove the hundred miles to Hartley Ranch in Pinon Hills and spent a couple of hours with Mike and his wife, Ginny. He liked them right off the bat. Mike was open and honest with him about what he could expect from his horse. He also loved his tour of the Arabian portion of the ranch and what Ginny had to say to him about them. He decided he would buy his wife an Arabian horse and have

Ginny do the training so he would be able to ride with his wife someday. That's about the time the seed of a ranch of his own crept into his consciousness. He would love to have a place in the desert for his horses and for his family to visit for weekends where they could ride.

He remembered when Mike first started working with Cutter. He was gentle and firm at the same time, encouraging Cutter and giving him credit for doing what he asked of him. He never saw an ounce of mean-spiritedness in Mike. He was always kind to his boy. He took Cutter on trail rides to get him used to stepping outside his comfort zone and seeing different things too.

But Mike noticed Cutter would often stare at the cattle he had on the ranch for his cutting horses. It hadn't occurred to him to train Cutter for cutting cows until he watched him watching the cattle. He knew cutting cows was not something Esteban would be doing with his horse. Just for the fun of it, he put cows in the work arena one day and took Cutter in to see what he would do. History was made that day! Cutter was a superb cutting horse. He zeroed in on his cow, cut it from the herd, and refused to allow that cow back in the herd. He would get down on the cow, weaving from side to side with his front legs while his rear legs stayed planted in one position if the cow waivered direction. He would nearly drop to his knees on the front to keep up with that single cow and spin and turn on a dime and give you nine cents change back. He would stare at the cow until the cow just stood there quivering, afraid to move. He was a champion in the making! He talked to Esteban about it. Esteban agreed to let him try Cutter in competition. For the next four years, Cutter won every time he set his hoof in the ring with cows. He made his training fees back many times over. Esteban had multiple offers for Cutter, some at outrageous prices. But, how could one possibly sell something as precious as his "Caballo de mi Corazon?" Esteban couldn't think of life without his buddy. The more he thought about it, the more afraid he became. He hated to admit to himself, but he would have been just as upset about his son being missing as he was about his horse.

Once they landed at Los Angeles International Airport, they had to pass through another customs screening before Esteban and Stevie could get a limousine for the trip to San Juan Capistrano. Stevie fell asleep during the drive from the airport to their home. Esteban woke him when they pulled into their driveway.

Esteban and Stevie arrived home almost 30 hours after leaving Louisa's parents home. He had very little sleep on the plane. Esteban was too worried to sleep anyway. Stevie ran upstairs to his room while Esteban went to the kitchen to make a pot of coffee. He noticed the answering machine on the counter blinking. He clicked the play button and listened to the messages. The first few calls were junk calls trying to sell something. Then he got to the messages from Becky Howard. They caused him to pause. Why in the world was Becky Howard calling him? He jotted down her phone number and kept listening to messages.

Then he heard the Texas drawl of Merle demanding $100,000.00 for the safe return of his beloved Cutter! He checked the date on the machine for when that message came in. He realized he was far past the deadline of 48 hours to respond. He ran the timeline through his head. That would have come in the same day the housekeeper left on her vacation. Nobody heard that message until now. Esteban Garcia panicked. Was he too late to save his beloved Cutter?

CHAPTER | SEVENTEEN

John and Rhonda walked toward the highway with lighter steps after spotting the first car they'd seen in days. John hoped he could flag someone down that would take them to a police station. The road they traveled had ruts and peaks and valleys along the length of it.

They came over one rise about two miles from the highway when they saw two trucks traveling south. What caught their attention was the fact the first truck hauled a travel trailer that looked like the one that sat outside the mobile home. The second truck was hauling a four-horse trailer like the one that brought Cutter from Apple Valley. They squatted down so not to be visible. If that was the four guys who held them hostage, they were getting away! They were not close enough to see if there was a horse in that trailer or not.

John encouraged Rhonda to speed up as much as she could. The two trotted as far as they could and slowed to rest before picking up the pace again. They were at the highway sooner than John thought they would be.

They looked like they'd been through a war. Neither had bathed in days. The desert dust clung to their damp skin, leaving tracks where sweat poured from their unprotected heads. Sweat and dirt left stains on their clothing. Rhonda's long silky hair was now dreadlocks coated in dust. And they were exhausted from the trek across miles of desert. John worried they might not be able to get someone to stop for them.

He saw a large truck approaching from the south and took a chance. John jumped out in the roadway in front of the truck and waved both his arms in the air. He was about a quarter of a mile from the truck when he made his leap. The driver put his brakes on immediately. He saw the woman standing beside the road. The man jumped out of the way. The driver pulled to the side of the road a short distance from the couple. He opened the passenger door on his cab and leaned out.

"You two in trouble?" he shouted.

Despite their exhaustion, John and Rhonda sprinted toward the truck cab. "Can we get a ride to the nearest police station?" John asked and had to stop and grab his knees to breathe. Rhonda grabbed the doorframe of the truck for support.

"Are you two okay?" the driver asked again.

"Yes, and no," John coughed out. "We were taken as hostages during a crime and we need to talk to the police as soon as possible. Will you give us a ride to the nearest police station?"

"Climb on in," the driver said. "Can I get you anything? Do you need water? By the way, my name's Red."

John helped Rhonda step up into the cab of the truck. He climbed in and sat beside her. Red handed them each a bottle of cold water from the cooler he kept behind the passenger seat in his cab. "If she needs to lie down, there's a bed in the back."

Rhonda was more exhausted than she'd ever been in her life. She took his offer of a place to lie down and crawled between the seats and fell fast asleep on the bed. "Thank you so much for stopping for us," John told him. "Would you be willing to drop us off at the nearest police station? I don't even know where we are."

"We're about 30 miles south of Ridgecrest, give or take a mile," Red said. "I'd be glad to take you there. I think I know where the Kern County Sheriff's Office is. Let's get this truck back on the road!"

Red put the big rig in gear, checked his mirrors for clearance and pulled the huge truck onto the highway. He turned off the radio and chatted with John as they drove. John filled him in on what happened to him and his wife as the big diesel engine pulled it's 80 thousand pound load up hills and down into arroyos along the desert highway. Soon they began to see small homes along the road, a few trees planted in yards, and other appearances of civilization. At the end of one long sweeping curve, the city of Ridgecrest came into view. Red expertly downshifted gears to slow the truck as they pulled off the highway onto the main road and headed into town. The sheriff's office was not too far from the highway. Red pulled his rig to a stop across the street from the office and shut off the engine. There was a quaint coffee shop beside the road. "Might as well take a rest stop and get something to eat before I get back on the road. I'm heading for St. George, Utah and then Denver. Can I buy you two something to eat before you talk to the sheriff? You look like you could use a meal."

John and Rhonda gratefully accepted Red's invitation. The three of them sat in a booth and had coffee, then breakfast as they talked. "I've been a long haul trucker for 25 years now, and I've seen a lot of people alongside the highway. But I have to admit I've never picked up a hostage before," he laughed. "At least I'll have a new story to tell my wife when I call her tonight. She's not going to believe me!"

Rhonda, a little energized after her short nap in the truck and decent food in her belly, suggested, "If you have one of those fancy phones, why don't you take our picture so you can show her? Maybe she'll believe you then. We must look a sight right now."

Red did exactly that. After he took their picture, he asked "Why don't you give me your phone number? I'd like to call you in a couple of days and make sure you are okay."

After Red paid the check for breakfast, the grateful couple thanked him profusely and walked with him back to his truck. As Red took off down the road, they walked across the street to the sheriff's office. They walked up to the service counter and waited while the deputy on duty finished a phone call. The deputy walked to the counter and asked, "May I help you?"

John cleared his throat and said, "Yes, we need to talk to someone. We were taken hostage from a ranch in Apple Valley eight or nine days ago we think. We escaped last night. Can you help us?"

CHAPTER | EIGHTEEN

The deputy at the service desk escorted John and Rhonda into an interview room at the sheriff's office. He asked them to wait a few minutes while he got a detective in to speak with them. He offered them coffee, soft drinks or water which they both declined. When the deputy left the room, Rhonda spread her forearms out on the table, overlapped her hands and dropped her head on them. Her exhaustion won. John sat beside her for five minutes before joining her in sleep.

They were startled awake about 45 minutes later when a plainclothes officer opened the door and entered. "Hi, sorry it took so long. I'm Detective Ron Evers. I understand you need to talk to someone about a crime you were involved in?"

John jumped to his feet and took the offered hand to shake. "I'm John Powell, and this is my wife, Rhonda," he told the detective. "Yes, we were involved in a crime. We need some help."

The detective pulled out a chair on the opposite side of the table, "Let's sit down and you tell me all about it." He pulled a pen out of his shirt pocket and began writing their names down in his notebook.

John told everything he knew from the time he and Rhonda heard a noise outside their cottage to when they walked into the sheriff's office. It took him a while. Every once in a while Rhonda added a detail or two. The detective scribbled wildly in his notebook and asked them to repeat many details of their experience. Rhonda gave him the Texas license plate number that she saw that night as they climbed into the truck bed. " 'I ate three times before six' helped me remember the last four numbers of the license plate, 8346, on the truck that pulled the horse trailer," she told him. She admitted they forgot to check the plate on the other truck in their haste to get away the night they finally picked the locks on the handcuffs. They each showed their wrist to the detective, showing the bruises and raw marks on their skin.

"That's some story, John," Detective Ron said when they finished their narrative. "So you believe the four men came to the Hacienda Rancho to steal Cut It Out and hold him for ransom? And you and Rhonda interrupted their scheme, so they took you along for the ride?

Do you have any idea how they communicated their ransom demand to the owner? You also said the owner is not even in this country now because the family went to Spain on a family emergency? Is that essentially correct?"

"That about sums it up," John admitted. "Sounds like a pretty strange story even to me."

Rhonda was mad. "Yes! That's what really happened! We've been strung up to a cast iron headboard for days and days. Those clowns forced us out of our home at gunpoint for their stupid get-rich-quick scheme. I'm worried about the five horses left there with no provision for food and water, and in this heat too! We've got to get back to the ranch. We don't have any money with us. We were forced to leave our cell phones there so we can't even call anyone! What are we supposed to do now?"

Detective Ron was taken aback by the anger she displayed. Up to this point, Rhonda had been fairly mild-mannered. "I see your point, Rhonda. The actual crime took place in San Bernardino County. You are sitting in Kern County where the thieves took you and the horse. So part of the crime took place here because you two were held against your will here as well as the horse who is stolen property. I'm going to have to reach out to the San Bernardino County Sheriff's Department for some help and cooperation. I know you're going to have to tell your story to them as well, same as you did here. Let me get on the phone and make some calls. I can probably get a San Bernardino County Deputy up here to pick you up and take you back home after they get a full report from you there."

"Those horses we get paid to take care of could be dying right now!" Rhonda nearly shouted. "We can't just sit here and talk while they die!"

"I understand your concerns. Let me make a few phone calls. I'll be back in a couple of minutes. Is there anything I can get you in the meantime?" the detective asked her.

"Not unless you can find me some clothes to wear and a hot shower," Rhonda snapped back.

John stepped in. "Honey, we have to help these people find those four creeps. I'm worried about the horses at the ranch too. Let Ron do his job and we'll get through all this sooner, okay?"

Rhonda slumped defeated in her chair. She never got riled up like that. It must be the exhaustion she felt. She was slightly ashamed of herself for snapping at the detective. She'd hold her tongue in the future. She laid her forearms on the table and crossed her hands again, dropped her head down and closed her eyes. Sleep would be wonderful. Sleep in her bed at home would be heavenly.

"Good news," Ron said when he came back in the interrogation room a few minutes later. "I talked to the watch commander at the Apple Valley station. They were at the ranch not long ago. They got a call a few hours ago because someone went to your ranch to check on the horses there and found the stallion missing and the door to the caretaker's cottage open. It looked suspicious to them. They permitted a Mike Hartley to remove the horses to his ranch in Pinon Hills. Five horses were taken there for medical evaluation and care."

Rhonda teared up. "Thank goodness. Mike and Ginny will take good care of them until we can get there."

"You know this Mike Hartley?" Ron asked.

John smiled broadly. "We sure do! We both worked for him. He was the one that recommended us to the owner of the ranch we work for now. It was a great job for us. Which brings up another situation. We need to reach the owner right away. He's in Spain with his family. He doesn't have any idea that his precious stallion is missing. That horse is his most prized possession, after his family of course."

"Well, I got more good news for you. There is a San Bernardino County Deputy on his way here to pick you up. He was already close to the county line. The watch commander redirected him here. He's to take you directly to the Apple Valley station. They may have more information before you get back there. I gave him the short version of what you told me here so they can start putting the puzzle pieces back together."

"Is there any way I could get a taco?" Rhonda asked. "I got this sudden craving for one. Would that be possible?"

"There's a little café across the street. They have a great Mexican cook in the back. He makes great breakfasts, but he makes wonderful lunches too. He serves the best little street tacos you've ever eaten. I'll have some brought over for you. John, you want some too or would you like a terrific wet burrito that weighs about a pound and a half?"

"That sounds wonderful!" John said and noticed his stomach was growling all of a sudden. What little they ate while captive never suited their tastes. Everything seemed soaked in grease. It was all they could do to get it down. They were looking forward to something decent to eat. Breakfast had been hours ago with Red, the trucker.

CHAPTER | NINETEEN

Once Doc Martin left the ranch and Ginny posted the feeding chart for the five rescued horses in the barn, she, Uncle Mike and Charles Carnegie left the barn and sat on the patio having iced tea and talking about the situation. That left Maryann and Brody in the barn. Clyde, Brody's black Labrador retriever, came and joined them laying in the middle of the barn aisle between them.

"I had no idea she would really remember you," Maryann told Brody. "Guess horses have long memories after all." Clyde sat up and whined for emphasis.

"You have no idea how nice it is to see her again," Brody admitted. "I've missed her every day since she left. Guess I didn't realize how big a hole that left in my heart either. Isn't she special?"

"Yes, she's beautiful. You really should have talked to your aunt and uncle and told them how you felt about her. Don't you see how much they love you? They would have tried their best to keep you two together."

"I told you how I felt about that. Aunt Ginny and Uncle Mike have been very good to me. I could have ended up an orphan in foster care. They took me in and became my guardians. Then they even adopted me. I have real parents legally. That's a lot for them to do. They've been so good to me it's hard to ask for more of them." Brody told her.

"It's okay to ask when it is something really special, you big dummy," she informed him. "Aunt Ginny and Uncle Mike really could afford to get you your horse. I'd even talk to my grandpa about helping. Becky is willing to ask her parents for help too. You are our friend and you've always been. You do so much to help us. I don't know if you realize it. Take me for example. When I first came here to work off riding lessons, I didn't know anything. I was scared to ask questions and scared I'd do the wrong things. You stepped up and helped me and taught me and made the work fun for me. You have no idea what that meant to me. I'd wanted to be with real horses since I could remember. You helped make that possible. I can't thank you enough! You're my best friend! You've stepped up and helped me when no one else our age would. And look at all the work you did at the national championship show. You were everywhere helping all of us with our horses, our tack, bathing and grooming, making sure the numbers were correct and a hundred different things. You should have been there showing with us, but you are too stupid to ask your parents for your own horse because you think they've done too much for you already! Get real! I want to go to the national show next year, and I want to be showing with you. Then there was all the help you did while we were stuck because of the fire. Who was the one who got the satellite phone working so we could let our parents know we were okay? That would be you again! Who was the one who organized the stuff that came out of the dropped supplies? That would be you again! Who was the one in that canyon who helped Hilda organize our circle chats so we'd stop being scared? That would be you! You gotta give yourself some credit, you know."

"Okay! Okay!" he looked her in the eyes. "You might be right on some of that. What I'd like to do is learn enough so I can take over the ranch when Aunt Ginny and Uncle Mike want to retire. I have a few years before that happens but I'd love to know what Uncle Mike does, why he does it, and how he does it so I can keep the ranch running the same way. Maybe I'll get lucky and marry me some girl who loves Arabian horses so she can take over Aunt Ginny's side of the ranch. I've already found a spot on the property where I can see building a home for my family someday."

"You taking applications for that girl who loves Arabians already?" Maryann laughed out loud.

"What's so funny about thinking ahead?" he asked as if his feelings were hurt.

"You! You're what's so funny. You don't even have whiskers yet and you're taking applications for a wife – Must Love Arabian Horses – so you can run this ranch," she laughed until her sides ached. "Come on, let's go groom your sweetheart of the day. I bet she'd love a good brushing. Maybe we can bathe her and her mom tomorrow."

"Please do me one favor, Maryann. Please don't say anything about what I just told you. I think I should talk to Uncle Mike and Aunt Ginny about it myself first. Who knows, maybe they planned to sell the ranch and move into some condo by the beach somewhere. We've never talked about it. But if it's possible, I'd like to take over for them someday and raise my own family here. I wouldn't want them to hear that from anyone but me when the time is right."

"I'm your friend," she replied. "I can keep secrets. I will never tell anyone about this – pinky promise!"

Brody and Maryann spent nearly an hour brushing Rosie down, picking the wind twists out of her mane and tail, and using the salve Uncle Mike liked on her rub spots. She was so bony that everywhere she came in contact with the desert soil rubbed the hair off and caused abrasions to her skin. They were shallow abrasions, not nearly as bad as the wounds Prince Ali came in with after the cougar attack in the mountains. They would heal in a few days. Once they finished up and picked out her feet with a hoof pick, they left her stall and gave her a couple more horse cookies to keep her busy while they did the same thing for her mother.

Once they finished grooming Desert Fire, Brody and Maryann left the barn to get a glass of iced tea and take a break on the back patio. Clyde was sleeping in the center of the aisle but woke when they left the barn.

"Hey, Rosie! Remember me?" Clyde asked her.

"Of course, Clyde. You and I used to chase each other around the arena when I was a little one," she answered. *"How could I forget you?"*

"Well, to be precise, I let you chase me around the arena, remember? If I had chased you I would have been booted off the place for tormenting the horses," he laughed. *"And you would never catch me now! What the devil happened to you? I saw you when you left here, but you look like you had a rough time wherever you went."*

Rosie told him all about the last ten days. Clyde whined in the sad spots, grinned his toothy grin with the tongue hanging out in the good ones, and wagged his tail at the end. *"Glad you are here again. Just don't try chasing me. I'm too old to run and you're probably going to catch me now. It's good to see you here again. Have to admit I missed you almost as much as Brody did."*

CHAPTER | TWENTY

The four men in the two trucks found the freeway interchange and switched direction from south to east on Interstate 10. They crossed the Arizona border at Blythe and continued toward the cutoff for Wickenburg, Arizona. There, they would change direction again heading north to Prescott, Arizona. After stopping for gas and food across the border, they found a rest stop and stayed the night in the travel trailer before pushing onward. The trucks rolled into Prescott the following day. It was a weekday just three days before the rodeo was scheduled to start. They found work on the grounds helping with the final set up of grandstand seating, animal pens, feeding animals, and whatever they could do for a few dollars an hour. By the time the rodeo opened for business on Friday night, they'd picked their spots and entered the events they hoped would make them even more money so they could push on to Texas at the close of the rodeo. They had prime parking in the lot because they were early to arrive. They parked the two trucks side by side and detached the horse trailer so they could use that truck for going into town when they needed supplies. Merle, of course, never made that phone call to anyone telling them where to find Cutter. He hoped the others would forget about it. He wanted to forget the whole episode.

****

Deputy Robert Johnston showed up at the Kern County Sheriff's Office an hour after Detective Ron Evers promised John and Rhonda he was coming to get them. They'd had a wonderful meal in the meantime and rested in the air-conditioned comfort of the station in Ridgecrest. Since they'd heard the five horses left at the Hacienda Rancho went to Mike Hartley's ranch in Pinon Hills for medical care, they weren't so worried about them. They did, however, wonder if Cutter was in that horse trailer they saw early that morning and worried he might have been left behind at the mobile home they'd just escaped from. It was a nagging little worry for the moment since they couldn't be sure.

Deputy Bob was a great guy. He chatted with them all the way back to Apple Valley to the Sheriff's Substation there. His wife had an Arabian horse she called Apollo. He said she liked that horse more than him sometimes. The three chatted amiably during the drive. Rhonda was most interested in the Arabians. John loved the Reining and Cutting horses which were generally American Quarter Horses or Paints. But, as John said, they all had four legs and a tail, so there were similarities to enjoy, no matter what breed someone preferred.

Two hours after they left Ridgecrest, Deputy Bob's patrol car turned into the parking lot of the San Bernardino County Sheriff's station in Apple Valley. He walked them into an interview room, gave them both a cup of coffee and left to find the sergeant and the detective who were waiting for the

Powells. He gave them his impressions of the couple before they met with them in the interview room.

The two officers joined John and Rhonda in the interview room, introduced themselves and asked their permission to record the conversation. The Powells had no objections. They pressed the record button on the recorder, pulled out their notepads and began the interview. John told them everything from the minute he and Rhonda heard a slight commotion in the barn area the night Cutter was stolen to the minute they arrived at the sheriff's office in Ridgecrest. Rhonda added in a few comments along the way. Both of the San Bernardino County officers had spoken with the Kern County officers while John and Rhonda were being driven back to Apple Valley. The stories were the same, and the couple seemed earnest and sincere. The officers interviewing them had no reason to disbelieve them.

"So you saw the two trucks with the travel trailer and the horse trailer heading south along the highway before you reached it?" the detective asked.

"Sure did," John said. "We were maybe two miles from the highway at the time. We were hoping they didn't see us. We weren't close enough to tell if the horse was in the trailer though. We're very concerned about him. He is our boss's prized stallion. He loves that horse. I've been working with him myself. I am fond of him too. I don't want anything to happen to him. He's an innocent victim here."

A bit agitated, Rhonda interjected, "We overheard one conversation the four guys had where they talked about leaving us handcuffed to the bed and leaving the horse in the corral and driving off. They actually talked about leaving us there to die of thirst or hunger while they got away, the heartless jerks!"

"Tell me what you know about Mike Hartley," the detective asked.

John looked at him questioningly, "He was our boss for about a year. He owns and runs a very nice spread in Pinon Hills. He's the one who trained Cutter. I understand he is now taking care of the five other horses who were left on the ranch. What do you want to know about him? He's a good guy! He will not have any part in this if that's what you're asking me."

"Are you sure he wouldn't be involved in this? We understand the missing horse is worth a lot of money. You don't think he would work with the other men to take him for some reason?"

Rhonda's eyes flew open at the suggestion, and her face began to turn red in anger. "Are you asking us what I think you are? Are you suggesting Mike or his wife would have anything to do with this? They are some of the most decent, hard-working people you will ever meet! I can't believe you'd even ask a question like that," she spat.

John, equally upset over the line of questioning, put his hand over Rhonda's balled fist on the table. "Sweetheart, I'm sure they have to ask these questions. Try not to get so upset and answer them honestly. Everything is going to be okay."

The detective softened his tone. "I'm sorry, but we do have to ask. We have a crime to solve here, and you two are our only witnesses. We've already checked the Hartleys out. They have a clean record and a high degree of credibility in the community. Thank you for your honesty with us. We have a few more questions for you; then we can wrap this up. Deputy Johnston will take you back home when we finish here."

John visibly relaxed. Rhonda flattened her hand out and rested it palm side down on the table top. She was still upset, but no longer furious with the tone and the line of questioning. "We do need to get home so we can call Mr. Garcia, the owner. He's in Spain with a family emergency. His wife's mother is very ill. They flew to Spain about a month and a half ago to help care for her. He has no idea what's been going on here. I would call him right now, but we left our cell phones at home. I've got to charge one up so we can get the phone number and call him. This is not a call I want to make," John admitted.

"I'll need that number for our files as well," the detective told him. "We need to talk to him too."

The interview finished up fairly soon after that exchange. Deputy Johnston drove John and Rhonda back to the ranch in Apple Valley and dropped them off before heading for home.

John walked into the caretaker's cottage first, leaving Rhonda on the porch outside while he checked it over to be sure there weren't any uninvited visitors inside. When he told her it was safe to enter, she headed straight to the shower, dropping her clothing on the floor as she went. She turned the water to as hot as she could stand it, stepped into the shower and stood there for a half hour before washing her face, hair, and body. Her skin was pink from the heat when she stepped out and wrapped her hair, then herself in towels and walked into the kitchen for a cold drink from the refrigerator.

John put the cell phones on the chargers while his wife showered. He sat on the patio with a cold drink and reflected on the past few days. He was filthy dirty, smelled, and was more tired than he'd ever been in his life. He nearly nodded off until his wife came outside still wrapped in towels to let him know, "It's your turn. You stink! You'll feel much better after a shower."

He returned to the patio 20 minutes later, clean and refreshed. "What do we do first?" she asked him.

"I think we should talk to Mike Hartley first. He was here earlier today and took the five horses back to his place. I'd like to get all the facts before I talk to Esteban."

"Good idea," she said as she handed him his cell phone. "Talk to Mike and see how the horses are."

CHAPTER | TWENTY-ONE

The Kern County Sheriff's Office placed an all points bulletin out for the partial Texas plate they'd gotten from Rhonda. They included the description of the truck and indicated it might be hauling a horse trailer with it.

The San Bernardino County Sheriff's Office placed an additional all points bulletin out for the same partial Texas plate with the description of the truck and trailer and expanded the search to cover the states of Arizona, New Mexico, and Texas in the hope of catching them before they got too far away. All state highway patrol divisions got a copy of the bulletin. The sheriff's office thought about this bulletin about an hour later and expanded it to include Nevada, Utah, and Colorado as well. In the supplemental bulletin they issued, they included a description of the missing stallion they'd gotten from John Powell.

A call came in the following morning from a highway patrolman in Arizona who saw the bulletin when he got back from his shift. He cruised through a rest area and thought he saw the truck and horse trailer there. The horse trailer had a Texas plate on it, but he had no reason to run the plate until he saw the bulletin. He never looked at the truck plate which was hidden behind the trailer. The California deputy who took his call asked him if the trailer had a horse inside. The Arizona officer was pretty sure the trailer was empty. The deputy reported the call to the detective assigned to the case. If the horse trailer was empty in Arizona, it probably left California that way. That meant Cutter had been left behind at the mobile home where the four men squatted waiting for their ransom money. He was in dire jeopardy.

****

John talked to Mike Hartley on the phone. After a general description of what happened to him and Rhonda, John asked Mike about the five horses he'd picked up at the ranch. Mike let him know Doc Martin checked them over and pulled blood. He gave them a re-feeding diet for the next few weeks and would have blood results back in the morning.

"I also called Esteban Garcia as soon as I could. I had a cell phone number for him, so I tried that. He called me back pretty quickly. He and his son Stevie are on their way home now. Esteban told me it would take at least 26 hours to get here with the flight, customs inspections, drive to the airport in Madrid and the trip from Los Angeles back to San Juan Capistrano. I don't expect to hear from him again until tomorrow," Mike told John.

"That saves me a call, then," John replied. "I was going to call you first and then call him with everything we know. I'll wait until he gets back to the states and talk to him then. Rhonda and I will be out to your place in the morning to see the other five. I think we're just going to turn in. We've not had a decent night's sleep for days now, and we walked all night last night. We're dead on our feet."

"Come for breakfast then," Mike suggested. "I'll let Ginny know you're coming. We can catch up over a decent meal and coffee."

CHAPTER | TWENTY-TWO

Friday night at the rodeo in Prescott added up to another eighty bucks for the men. Pat had his first ride in the bronc division. He was good enough to hang in there long enough for points and got dumped pretty hard coming off the stallion. He bruised his right shoulder but it wouldn't stop him from riding again on Saturday. His buddies met him at the gate, and they walked to the concession area for something cold to drink.

"If our luck holds like this," Merle said cheerfully, "we'll have enough to get back home with spare cash in our pockets for a change."

Pat laughed. "That ground is hard out there guys. Watch yourselves. I'd love to get home with a few dollars left so I can take a day or two to heal up before we have to get to work again.

****

The detective working the case in Apple Valley got a call from the deputy who talked to the Arizona highway patrol officer. He got the highway patrol officer's phone number and called him back right away. After he identified himself, he asked, "Are you sure the horse trailer was empty?"

The Arizona officer thought about it for a half a second, "I think it was empty. Usually, you see urine or horse poop coming out the back of those trailers if they've been on the road for a while. I've seen enough of them on Interstate 10. There was nothing like that on this trailer. I didn't see any motion or hear anything from inside it either. Those stock trailers make a racket when livestock inside moves around. Why is this important?"

"To be honest with you, we have a half million dollar horse missing right now. If he is in that horse trailer, at least we know where he is. If he's not in that trailer, he's most likely been abandoned out here in the Mojave Desert. We're going to have to find him very quickly, or we may not find him alive."

"Oh, wow, I had no idea. Was the truck and horse trailer traveling with another vehicle of any kind? The one I saw at the rest stop was parked right next to another truck towing a travel trailer. Could this be your guys?"

"It sure could!" the detective said. "Is there any chance you got a license on film from your dash camera when you drove through that parking lot? We have the last four numbers of the truck plate for one of the trucks. We're assuming they are both from Texas and our witnesses were not sure of the year for either of them. They confirmed they are both Dodge trucks made in the late 1990's. One of the trucks was pale or very faded yellow. The other was a faded metallic green on the top with a gray bottom. The yellow truck had a smear of red paint on the driver's door, both were extended cab trucks, and the yellow one hauled the horse trailer.

"That sounds like your trucks, alright," the highway patrol officer confirmed. "Let me get with my supervisor and see if we can find the tags on my dash cam video. I may have been turned toward them when I drove into the parking area. Maybe we'll get lucky. Give me your number. I'll get back to you in a few minutes."

Twenty minutes later the Arizona highway patrol officer called back. "We got a partial plate on the horse trailer. That plate is crunched in and we couldn't read the first number. What we did get is a trailer plate with 331 C on it without the first number. The travel trailer plate was in better condition. It was definitely a Texas trailer plate 4786 H. We were able to confirm the approximate year and make on the trucks. The color did match what you gave me. We looked closely at the horse trailer in the video. We can't see a horse in there."

"Thank you very much. I will modify our all points bulletins with this information. Can you make the change in your department? These guys are still in the wind. We need to find them. By this time they could be almost anywhere. They stole a valuable horse and tried to ransom him. They took two people hostage that tried to stop them. They held them at gunpoint and chained up for eight or nine days. If they didn't take the horse with them, they've left him out in the desert with no protection and possibly no food or water."

"I'm a horse lover myself," the Arizona officer admitted. "I hate horse abusers! What they did was plain horse abuse. We'll find them if I have anything to say about it!"

CHAPTER | TWENTY-THREE

John and Rhonda got up in the morning at their usual time and had nothing to do at the ranch. Most of the horses were at Hartley Ranch, and they had an invitation for breakfast there. They showed up in time to sit at Ginny's kitchen table with her, Mike and Brody for coffee and breakfast. They told the Hartleys all about what happened to them up until they got home last night. Their concern still was the location of Cutter. They were too far away from the highway to see if Cutter was in the horse trailer heading south the morning after their escape.

Mike was equally concerned about the horse. He'd spent a lot of time with that horse and built a great relationship with him. They were wildly successful together. He didn't want anything bad to happen to him.

"Do you think you could pinpoint where they kept you?" Mike asked.

"It was dark when we got there, we were laying in the back of an open pick-up bed, and rushed into the house when we got there," John explained. "When we finally got the handcuffs off, we jumped out the window and had no idea where we were. The only thing going for us that night was a full moon. We walked and listened hoping to hear the sound of traffic. I don't even really know which direction we were going. We did see a cutoff from the main highway to a place called Trona when the officer drove us back to Apple Valley. We don't know if we were held off that road or the main highway," John admitted. "The trucker who picked us up said it was about 30 miles to Ridgecrest when he picked us up. That's about as much as I know. But I would assume we were on the main highway since it was a long haul trucker that picked us up."

Rhonda looked pensive for a minute then said, "We really couldn't see that much until closer to dawn. It felt like we walked a hundred miles, but we know it couldn't have been. We're not sure what time we left the trailer. Neither of us had a watch or cell phone to check. It's so hard to gauge time under those circumstances."

The group finished breakfast and went to the barn. Rhonda and John wanted to see the five horses on the Hartley Ranch and see to their comfort. They were appalled at how thin the horses were but even more glad they were with Mike and Ginny after seeing them. Ginny filled them in on the part Maryann Wilcox and her grandfather played in getting them to safety.

"We need to meet those two and thank them. When we got back to the ranch last night, it was all we could do to shower and fall in bed. I'm so grateful they took the time to check on them," Rhonda said.

"You'll meet them soon enough," Ginny told her. "Maryann comes over every day with her mom, her grandmother or her grandfather. She used to come here to work off riding lessons but that all changed a couple of months ago. She never met her grandparents and they didn't know she existed. She and her mother are being well cared for now. Maryann is a good friend of Brody's. She's quite an accomplished rider too. We'll have to tell you about the Youth Nationals Show sometime, and the detour we made to Colorado afterward. That was quite an ordeal."

Brody walked into Rosie's stall and began scratching her withers gently. Rosie, if she could, would have been purring. Since she couldn't purr, she was letting out little squeals like a baby horse, pressing her skin into his fingers as he worked on her.

"What in the world is that?" Rhonda asked when she heard the little squeals.

"That's Rosie. Apparently, she and Brody had an attachment none of us knew about before she went home. She's been like this since she spotted Brody when we took her off the trailer," Ginny told her.

"Oh, my, I've never heard her act like that," Rhonda whispered while looking in the stall. "She's always been a favorite of mine, but I've never seen anything like this." Rhonda stood and watched Brody and Rosie. Rosie's eyes were closed and the little squealing sounds kept coming. Brody didn't notice anyone there and was intent on rubbing her withers and neck, massaging her muscles as he went. He worked all down her spine to her tailbone and massaged the muscles down the back of her legs in turn.

Rhonda turned to Ginny, "Would you loan him to me? I'd love a massage like that myself! After walking all night and being tied up for days, my muscles are a bit knotted up too." She giggled.

Ginny laughed under her breath. "I don't know. I think this relationship began in babyhood sometime. You might have to get yourself a professional."

Brody walked down the opposite side of Rosie, massaging her muscles on that side like he did the first and ended up stroking her cheek. Then he did something unexpected. He plopped two fingers into her mouth. She squealed a little, then began sucking on them loudly, making slurping noises.

Brody and Rosie were in their own little world and had not noticed the two women watching them through the top of the stall. He talked to Rosie in low tones, "Easy Rosie, don't bite. Remember, I showed you how not to bite my fingers. It's okay to suck on them if you want, just don't bite me."

Rhonda looked at Ginny with her eyes wide open and her mouth in a perfect "O". Ginny looked just as surprised as she was. "Well, I've never seen that before either," she admitted.

Brody suddenly saw the women out of the corner of his eye and pulled his fingers out of Rosie's mouth. "Uh, I'm sorry. I didn't know you were there," he stammered. He patted Rosie on her neck and stepped out of the stall a bit red in the face.

"What in the world were you doing?" Ginny asked him.

"It's just a game Rosie and I played when she was little. I read up on it and found out that baby horses suck on their mother 104 times a day on average. Her mother acted like she was a little tired of being sucked on sometimes and pushed Rosie away. I felt sorry for her and let her suck on my fingers. I wouldn't want any baby sucking on a part of me 104 times a day either. It was okay until she grew teeth. I had to teach her not to bite me. She was always good about that. She remembered it too." He was embarrassed at being caught in the act.

Brody, a little shamefaced, walked to the other end of the barn where Uncle Mike and John were talking about the other horses. The barn phone rang. Mike stepped into the office to answer it. He talked on the phone for a few minutes before hanging up and returning to the barn aisle.

"That was the detective from Apple Valley working this case. They think the men who stole Cutter and held you captive were in Arizona last night. The Arizona Highway patrol spotted their vehicles before they got the all points bulletin. They had no reason to search them at the time, so they didn't. But the officer who spotted the trucks and trailers is pretty sure there was no horse in the horse trailer. They would have difficulty crossing the Arizona border with the horse and no paperwork. That leads the detective, and me, to believe they left the horse where he was. He's going to be in trouble very soon if we can't find him."

"Oh, no!" John said. "We overheard them talking about leaving us handcuffed to the bed and leaving the horse there and just getting out of there. It sounds like they left Cutter when they found us gone. How are we going to tell Esteban Garcia that?"

CHAPTER | TWENTY-FOUR

Mike looked at his watch. "Ginny, what time did I get that call back from Esteban yesterday? Do you remember?"

She thought about it for a minute. "We'd already brought the horses here and unloaded them. You'd parked the trailer and came back to the barn. I'm guessing you called him close to 12:30 p.m. and he called you back within maybe 15 minutes, so 12:45 p.m. maybe?"

"He said he would be home in about 26 hours with the travel to and from airports, customs inspections at both ends, plus the flight time. That should put him back home in San Juan Capistrano by 3:00 p.m. today. If he's flown all night long, he may need a rest before he gets in the car to drive another two hours to get here. Depending, we could see him this evening or early tomorrow morning. Guess we'll have to wait to hear from him directly when he gets home."

"This is not a call I'm looking forward to," John muttered under his breath. "How are we going to tell him Cutter is out in the desert somewhere, maybe without shelter, food or water, and we don't know where he is or how to get to him?"

"Let's get the detective back on the phone and see what kind of help the sheriff's people can give us. Do you have the phone number for the Kern County Sheriff's Office or the people there you and Rhonda talked to? Maybe they can help us some," Mike suggested. "This doesn't sound good at all."

John pulled a couple of business cards out of his wallet and showed them to Mike. "These are the numbers we got. Let's get on the phone."

John and Mike walked back into Ginny's office in the barn and made calls to both sheriff's offices. They explained their concerns and listened. They were not overly encouraged. It was a large desert and many square miles of land. The different counties had some cooperative skills and services they could offer but searching for a horse in such a vast area would be a challenge for either department with limited resources. They told their wives what they knew. They both felt hopeless in the situation, and neither of them wanted to give that news to Esteban Garcia.

Maryann and Charles Carnegie showed up at the ranch a few minutes later. Mike and Ginny introduced them to John and Rhonda Powell who were sincere in thanking them for what they'd done yesterday. "If you ever get that kind of "spidy-sense" again, I want you to promise me you'll tell me about it too," Ginny told Maryann.

"Aunt Ginny, it's not "spidy-sense". I just got worried about Desert Rose. I knew how much Brody loves that mare. When we couldn't get anyone to call us back, I got worried and wanted to make sure she was okay," Maryann explained.

"Your timing was excellent, young lady," Rhonda told her. "I'm glad you checked. I'm very glad they are here and safe right now. Thank you, and thank you too, Charles, for looking in on our charges when we couldn't."

105

"We're glad you two are okay. Things could have been so much worse," Charles said. "It's so nice to meet you two and see that you are okay. Anything could have happened out there in the desert as well. You could have disappeared forever."

The adults adjourned from the barn area to the back patio for iced tea. Brody and Maryann stayed in the barn. Brody went back to work on Rosie again while Maryann pulled La Duquesa out of her stall to groom her and get her ready to ride. As she brushed Quesa down, Maryann said, "It's a shame about Cutter. Do you think the sheriffs will be able to find him?"

"I've been out almost where they were taken going dirt biking with friends before. There's a whole lot of nothing out there. Every once in a while you come across a broken down property or an old mine shaft with an attempt to cover the hole, lots of rocks, lots of dirt, and not much else. I don't know how they're going to find Cutter. He's such a sweet horse, and Uncle Mike likes him so much. Mr. Garcia is going to be upset. He thinks that horse walks on water. I don't know if they will find him in time."

"Can't they take helicopters up and search from the air?" Maryann asked. "They do that for people don't they?"

"Sometimes they do, but they do it for people, not for a horse," Brody answered with a grim look. "They are not going to risk anyone else or put out a lot of money over a horse."

"But if they went up in a helicopter, couldn't they spot him so we could come pick him up?" she asked.

"Helicopters cost a lot of money. Fuel for helicopters costs a lot of money. I don't know if they will want to use them to search miles and miles of desert for a horse," Brody answered, frowning. "Most people think of a horse as just a horse. They don't think of them the same as people you know."

"How many batteries do you have for the whizzy drone you got for Christmas last year?" she asked him.

"What does that have to do with anything?" he questioned.

"If they won't send up a helicopter, maybe we could pin the area down on a map based on where John and Rhonda got to the highway and search the area with your drone. If you can fly it and have it transmit the photos to your laptop, I can watch the laptop, and we could maybe get the GSP coordinates for where he is when we find him. What do you think?" she asked.

"It's a long shot, but probably a better shot than Cutter has otherwise. I have several spare batteries, and we can charge them up with a car charger. We need someone to get us there to the search area and stay with us while we look for him."

"Okay, let's get to the house and look on your computer and see if we can pin down the search area first before we ask for a driver to take us," she suggested. "Maybe John or Rhonda can help us with that."

Brody and Maryann put their horses away and gave them treats before walking to the back patio to make their suggestion. The adults looked at them like they were crazy at first, but once they explained the technology and how they intended to handle it, it began to make some sense to them. Charles and John volunteered to go with the two youngsters on the search mission. They began making a list of supplies they needed to take with them, including food and water and maps. They knew they would have to end searching before dark because the drone did not have lights and Brody would not be able to manage it in the dark.

John and Rhonda come into Brody's room while he pulled up topographical maps of the general area so they could get an idea of where to begin the search. It looked so small on the monitor. When Maryann looked at the scale in miles, it began to sink in for her just how huge this project was. She needed to get home for her things and get back to the ranch with her grandfather with his Jeep gassed up and ready to go.

Brody spent that time putting together the equipment he would need for a search of that magnitude. Aunt Ginny put together a backpack with food and water for him and an extra one for the others. One of the adults would remain with Maryann at the car monitoring the photos and communicating with Brody while one would accompany Brody and his drone. Cell phones did not always work out in the desert so Brody brought along two extra radios that should cover the voids in communications with spare batteries for them as well. Charles was going to have to keep the Jeep running most of the time, so he brought extra gasoline for it in two five-gallon cans.

When they finished packing all the equipment and supplies in the Jeep, there was barely room for Maryann and Brody in the back seat, but they squeezed in. The Jeep was a pretty deluxe version which had numerous charger ports in back, front and in the console, so they plugged everything in they could to charge them up during the drive. Charles drove while John watched to find the dirt road they'd used to get to the highway. He remembered there was a tattered flag on a post on the south side of that road.

John pointed out the tattered flag as soon as he saw it. Charles slowed the Jeep and turned off the highway a short distance and stopped. John got out of the Jeep and looked ahead of it for slippered footprints he and his wife made on their way to the highway the day before. He found them! He rushed back to the Jeep and climbed in. "This is it!" he told them. "Let's take it up the road and see if we can find the campsite we came through. That would be a good place to begin the search."

They looked at several possible campsites before they found the one John and Rhonda left their slippered footprints through. They stopped the Jeep and began hauling equipment out. Brody took the drone out of its case and set it on the hood of the Jeep before turning it on. He turned the controller on and tested it with the drone. The drone lifted off the Jeep hood perfectly and hovered above the campsite while Maryann got the video up on the laptop. The picture was very clear, and the GPS coordinates showed in the lower corner of the monitor. Brody made sure he had his cell phone in his pocket and one of the radios on his belt. He and John began walking along the route that seemed right to John. They stopped about a hundred yards from the campsite and radioed back to the Jeep to be sure everything was working correctly. Maryann confirmed the video was great and everything seemed to be working perfectly.

John remembered the way from the day before fairly well at first. After the sun rose, their vision of their surroundings was more clear than they were before the sun came up. They moved well and found slippered footprints every once in a while for several hours. John kept an eye on the time. They were getting quite far from the campsite and would have to turn around to get back before the sun went down again. Brody sent the drone higher and in a wide arc above and in front of them searching. They saw nothing but dirt, rocks, desert plants and a few dirt bike tracks.

The farther they got from the campsite, the less sure John was of the direction they needed to go. He turned them around and headed for camp before it got too late for the search to continue that day. He was disappointed. He'd hoped this search would be easier than it was and he became more concerned they might not be able to find Cutter at all. He spotted another "road" of sorts that looked like it had been traveled on by vehicles other than dirt bikes. He had Brody check that road out with the drone and see if it connected to anything close to the campsite they were using as a base camp. It did! They could use that road to get farther into the desert with the Jeep, so he and Brody didn't have so far to walk back to camp. They could expand their search area better tomorrow.

The searchers packed up their gear and got back to the highway just before sunset. Nobody had much to say on the drive back to Hartley Ranch. Brody and Maryann felt they could find Cutter easily with the drone and laptop. They didn't realize how large their search area was and they knew every minute counted for Cutter. If Cutter was out of food, he could last a few days. If he was out of water, he couldn't.

CHAPTER | TWENTY-FIVE

Esteban Garcia leaned over the counter with his head in his hands. What should he do next? He thought about it for a few minutes, trying to clear his mind. He was tired from lack of sleep and worry. But he couldn't sit here in San Juan Capistrano doing nothing! He had to do something. He popped the tape out of the answering machine and pushed it deep in his pocket thinking how glad he was he'd not upgraded the machine to one of those all electronic ones that had no tapes. With his "old school" machine, he could give the tape to the sheriff's department as evidence. He hauled his bag upstairs to his bedroom and tossed most of what he'd brought home on the bed. He took his shaving kit and a change of clothes and stuffed them into a smaller case from his closet and walked down the hall to his son's bedroom.

"Come on, Stevie, we gotta go. I need you to drive me to Hartley Ranch."

"Really, Dad, you want me to drive you?" Stevie said with some enthusiasm. It was the first time his dad asked him to drive him anywhere since he took the driver's education course and prepared to take his license exam.

"You bet. You slept on the plane, and you slept most of the way home in the limo. I've not gotten any sleep so it would not be good for me to try a two-hour drive right now."

"Sure, Dad. Where are we going?"

"We're going to Mike and Ginny Hartley's place in Pinon Hills. I'll give you directions. I need to get there so I can be there while we figure out this mess with the horses and John and Rhonda. Okay? Bring a change of clothes. I don't know where we'll end up staying for the night."

Esteban and Stevie threw their small bags in the back seat of Esteban's car and climbed in. Esteban directed his son to the freeway and gave him directions as he drove. During a long stretch on the toll road, Esteban called Mike Hartley and told him they were on their way up to see him.

Ginny worried what to do with all the people. She knew John, Brody, Maryann, and Charles wanted to get back out in the desert early tomorrow to continue the search. That meant John and Rhonda needed a place to stay for the night. With Esteban and Stevie coming, they were not sure if they'd want to drive all the way to the Hacienda Rancho to spend the night and come back in the morning. She called Rose Wilcox, Maryann's mother and asked her if her guest room was open for the night. Ginny explained what was going on. Rose told her that her guest room was open and Charles and Celeste, Maryann's grandparents had one available too. In the crisis, everyone's door was open for family and friends. Ginny stopped worrying about that. Things would all sort themselves out the way they should.

Esteban and Stevie arrived at Hartley Ranch a few minutes before the searchers returned from the desert. Esteban had enough time to tell Mike about the ransom call that came in on his answering machine and pulled the tape out of his pocket to show Mike. Mike took him to his office and called the detective working the case. He explained who Esteban was and put him on the phone. Esteban told him about the ransom demand he'd found on his answering machine when he got home, told him he had the tape in his pocket to turn over to him, and gave him the phone number he was supposed to call to confirm he had the message and would comply with their demand. He had called the number from home. The phone rang a few times; then an automated voice came on saying the voice mailbox for the phone had not been set up and the call disconnected.

"But the phone number rang when you dialed it?" the detective asked him.

"Oh yes, it rang five times before going dead," Estaban explained. "I only called it once though."

"If this is a 'burner' phone and they realized you weren't going to call, they may have just left it in the old mobile home when they took off. I will have our people start working on that angle. If they just left it at the place where they were holding their hostages, there's a chance it still has some charge in the battery. If our people can figure out the service provider from the phone number and start chasing it down, maybe we can get a location by pinging the phone and getting it's GPS. That's good news. Let's hope it stays charged until we can ping it."

"That is maybe good news then?" Esteban sounded hopeful.

"Let's see what our people can find on that phone number. I'll let you know as soon as I find out anything."

Charles, John, Maryann, and Brody arrived back home shortly after Mr. Garcia made the call to the detective. Mike and Ginny introduced Charles Carnegie and Maryann. Esteban hugged them all and thanked them for what they were doing to help find his Cutter. He looked about ready to collapse so Ginny walked him to their guest room and insisted he get some sleep.

Brody looked at Stevie. "Hey, you want the top or the bottom bunk, your choice? You can stay with me in my room." Stevie grabbed his case and walked down the hall with Brody to his room. Brody looked up to Stevie. Stevie drove his dad's car on the freeway all the way from San Juan Capistrano to the ranch! Brody had driven farm vehicles around and parked the truck a few times but had never driven off the ranch before. He had to wait almost two years before he could apply for his driver's license. Stevie was a hero to him at that moment.

Charles drove Maryann home and dropped her off before heading up the mountain to his own home. John and Rhonda followed Charles home and spent the night with him and Celeste since John needed to be up early to begin the search in the morning with Charles and the two youngsters.

Stevie chose the bottom bunk and nearly fell into bed. It had been a tiring long day since he and his dad left Spain. He was nervous driving from home to the High Desert, and that exhausted him even more. He was asleep the minute his head hit the pillow. Brody had hoped to talk to him before going to bed himself but could see that wasn't going to happen. He left his room and closed the door behind him. He walked back to the kitchen to see what Aunt Ginny and Uncle Mike were doing. It was a tiring day for him too. He was disappointed they didn't find Cutter. He was concerned for the horse. He worried if he wasn't able to spot him tomorrow, they might not find him alive.

Ginny asked Brody to join her and Uncle Mike in the kitchen for a cup of coffee together. Ginny thought Brody showed a lot of maturity in the search for Cutter. She and Mike offered him more adult treatment than they'd given him in the past.

While Brody was busy adding cream and sugar to his cup, Ginny asked him, "Why didn't you tell us how you felt about Rosie before she went home? We had no idea you were so attached to her or we would have tried to make it possible for you to keep her."

He looked up from his cup while he stirred the sugar. "This is like a déjà vu conversation," he said. "I think I had this same conversation with Maryann."

"Well?"

"Okay, I'll tell you the same thing I told her. I've been so grateful to you and Uncle Mike for taking me in when I had no one, that I didn't feel right asking you for the luxury of my very own horse. You've already done so much for me. I would have ended up in foster care somewhere if you hadn't taken me home. My dad's parents were already gone, and my dad had no brothers or sisters. Your parents were much too old to raise a four-year-old, and you have no other sisters or brothers either. I was an orphan with no family but you and you took me in. You adopted me. I'm legally your son. How much more could I ask from you?"

"But we love you, Brody. We'd do anything to make you happy," Ginny said. Mike nodded his agreement without saying a word.

"I know you love me. You know, we three are the only ones that know what happened after the accident. I don't remember much about it; I remember we'd had a wonderful day at the ranch, good food, and I was getting sleepy after my dad pulled out on the highway. The last thing I remember clearly was my mother screaming. Then the world went crazy. When the car stopped moving, it was silent except for my brother whimpering. A strange man pulled me out through the window and held me as I cried. Then I heard the sirens and saw all the flashing lights, and I cried for my mommy. That man just held me and tried to comfort me. I remember the ride to the hospital in the ambulance with my brother, but he'd stopped whimpering. I remember you and Uncle Mike were there. I know I had nightmares about that for a long time and every time I cried, you'd come into my room and hold me until I stopped crying. You and Uncle Mike had no experience with children before you brought me home. I don't know how you did it. You have been my heroes."

"Brody, you were our family and family always does the best for family. If you don't take anything else from this experience, please remember this," Ginny said softly.

"Aunt Ginny, you and Uncle Mike didn't have to take me in, but I love and respect you for doing it. You know, Rosie went home two years ago. I've learned a few more things since then. I've learned that I love the ranch life. I have so many advantages other kids don't have. I get to see new life on the ranch when foals are born, when cows are born, when the barn cats have their kittens, when the hen's chicks hatch. I don't have time to spend on video games and playing on my phone all the time, but I've gotten to see life, the good and the bad. That is what I want for my children. I've been thinking I'd love to help Uncle Mike and you to run this ranch when you want to retire. I want to go to college at Cal Poly in Pomona like you both did so I don't have to leave here. I want to find me a wife who loves Arabian horses like you and I'd love to work with Uncle Mike to learn the why and the how and the what he does so I can do it and let you enjoy your old age knowing you've trained me to run things the way you did it. I've thought about this and even picked out a place on the ranch where I think I'd like to build a home to raise my own family. I know I'm almost 15, not 21, but I've been thinking about my future. And I'm so glad you took me in and gave me the opportunities you've given me." Brody's manner changed, and he grinned at his aunt, " Except I need a new Xbox so I can learn to beat the pants off Maryann. She's got the newest one. Speaking of Maryann, that girl is something else. You know this whole drone search for Cutter was her idea, don't you? She heard us talking, heard about Cutter and what's happening to him, and she put this all together. She's amazing. And she kills me with my games when we have time to play them."

Uncle Mike sat listening and was dumbfounded to hear what Brody had to say. He couldn't have been more proud of a son if he'd been born to him. He'd just heard what every father would love to hear, that his son wanted to follow in his footsteps. And he admired Brody for his ability to tell him and Ginny about it. Mike didn't think he'd had that kind of courage to speak with his father when he was Brody's age. But it all worked out for Mike. His older brother took over the business in Montana when their parents retired. He ran it into the ground because he wouldn't do things the way his parents did them. He lost everything. Fortunately, his parents didn't live to see the bank foreclosure. His brother took his family to Helena and got a job selling tires to support them. With Brody, he specifically said he wanted to know the what, why and how he and Ginny ran the ranch. If he found a better way, that was okay, but he'd at least have their foundation and he wanted it. He didn't think he was smarter than his parents, who couldn't possibly know anything, right off the bat the way his brother did. Mike felt his legacy was safe in Brody's hands – someday.

Mike drained his coffee cup and cleared his throat. He was never much for words. "I'm proud of you, son, and I love you very much." It was the first time Mike called him that.

Aunt Ginny pushed her cup aside, leaned over and kissed Brody on the forehead. "I'm proud of you too. And I love you. But it's time for you to get to bed. The others will be here early in the morning."

Clyde got up from his comfortable spot on the rug and wagged his tail as he followed Brody to his bedroom. Brody was tired. It had been a long day. It was still early, but he decided to get some sleep. Just as he turned the doorknob on his bedroom door, the phone in his pocket started ringing. He pulled it out of his pocket, saw it was Maryann, and answered, "Hello."

CHAPTER | TWENTY-SIX

The minute Maryann got home she dashed off to her bedroom and picked up the phone. She called Becky and filled her in on the day and the search for Cutter. "I think that was the first time I've ever seen a grown man cry," she told Becky. "Mr. Garcia is so upset about Cutter. I think he must feel about that horse the same way I feel about Quesa, and you feel about Ali. I can't imagine how I'd feel if someone dumped Quesa in the desert without food, water, or shelter. I'd be crazy frantic to find her. That's why tomorrow is so important. Brody and I talked about it after we got back today. With the updates we heard from the cops, Cutter may have been left out there two whole days already. Tomorrow will be three for him. If they didn't give him water, he could die before we find him. We have to find him!"

Becky was almost as upset as Maryann. "You know, Ali was out in the wilderness too, but I didn't know anything about it. I was in the hospital. Had I been up and around, I would have been nuts. I'm going to talk to Mom. I want to come up and help. It's only 7:30 pm now. If I can talk Mom into bringing me up, can I stay with you and go out on the search with you guys tomorrow?"

"Yeah! That would be great. Talk to your mom and let me know. I'll let my mom know."

Fifteen minutes later, Becky called Maryann back. "We're coming. We'll see you in a couple of hours. If mom doesn't want to drive back home tonight, can she stay in your guest room? I was also thinking, would it help at all if we had mounted riders out there looking for Cutter? If so, I'll bring Ali. Maybe we can get some other riders to help. What do you think?"

"I hadn't thought of that, but maybe. Yes, your mom can stay if she doesn't want to drive home tonight. I'll call Melissa, Kathy, Heidi, and Suzy and see if they want to ride out with you tomorrow. Maybe they can find John and Rhonda's tracks and follow them. The more I think about it, that's a capital idea. The more feet we have on the ground out there, the better our chances are of finding Cutter!"

While Becky and her mom were hauling Ali to Hartley Ranch, Maryann got on the phone with Brody. She filled him in on Becky's suggestion. "Can we make this work?" she asked.

"Let me talk to Aunt Ginny and Uncle Mike," he suggested. "They'd have to be involved. We'll need the big horse trailer and something to haul extra water for the animals. Based on what we saw out there today, I'd say that might work. Have you talked to the other girls yet? Will their parents let them do this?"

Brody rushed off to talk to Ginny and Mike while Maryann began calling the other girls. When Brody presented Maryann and Becky's suggestion, Mike and Ginny were hesitant at first. "That's a big desert out there with lots of hazards for the girls," Mike said.

"Uncle Mike, those girls are all national champion riders. They know what their horses will do. They will be covering ground that's used every weekend by kids on dirt bikes. If they can handle the terrain on a dirt bike, those horses certainly can. And, as Maryann said, the more feet we put on the ground, the better our chances are of finding Cutter in time."

Ginny sat with her head spinning. The logistics of getting enough horses and supplies out into the desert early tomorrow morning would be complicated. She sat down and started making a list of things that would be needed. It wasn't just a sack lunch of sandwiches for four people anymore. They would need the large trailer which held a hundred gallons of water in the tank, plus extra feed for horses, plus a lot more food for a lot more people. She checked her watch. It was only 8:15 pm. She picked up the phone and called Rose Wilcox, Maryann's mother. She briefed her on the new situation. She needed to go to the market in town for supplies for the people who would be searching, and she needed help putting it all together.

"Let me go to the store for you," Rose suggested. "I can do that on my way over there. I'll bring my Aunt Adele with me, and I'll call Maryann's grandmother. Between the four of us, we should be able to get the food ready tonight. Give me your list. I'll see you in about 45 minutes."

For an evening when things should have been calming down for the day, the pace picked up. Ginny finished putting her list of things needed other than the food for humans and went over it with Mike to be sure she didn't forget anything necessary. He added a halter and lead rope for Cutter. "We're going to need that when we find him!" he told her emphatically. They discussed which vehicles to take. "Charles' Jeep, of course, and our big truck and trailer need to go so we can haul the horses. We should have one or two other 4-wheel drive vehicles, and we'll need every handheld radio on the ranch."

"Can we find all ten of them?" Ginny asked. Mike nodded. "Then let's make sure they are all charged up tonight! You and I can round them up and get them on the chargers while I wait for Rose, Adele, and Celeste to get here." They dashed out the back door looking for radio units. Mike hooked them up on the charging station in Ginny's office. Mike checked the gas gauge on his big truck and drove it into town for a full load of gas. Brody checked off things on Ginny's list and stacked items in the barn aisle.

Rose, Adele, and Celeste arrived with bags of groceries. With Ginny's help, they turned the kitchen into a flurry of activity, making sandwiches, snack bags of cookies and crackers, washing fresh fruit and putting food in small baggies the searchers could take with them in saddlebags or backpacks.

By the time the food was prepared and stored in the refrigerator, Becky and Caroline Howard arrived with Prince Ali. Becky unloaded him and put him in a stall in the barn before coming to the house.

Brody came up from the barn with her. He'd found the last item on Ginny's list and added it to the pile.

By the time they got back to the patio, Ginny, Adele, Celeste, Rose, and Caroline were sitting down out there. Ginny popped back up and said, "How about a small glass of wine? I think that would be a wonderful idea." When they agreed, she went back into the house and came out with glasses on a tray with a bottle of uncorked wine, filled the glasses, and offered a toast. Here's to finding Cutter tomorrow!" While the ladies enjoyed their drinks on the patio, Mike came and got Caroline's keys. He parked and unhooked her horse trailer and parked her truck in the driveway beside Rose's and Celeste's Jeeps.

He sat with the women and said, "We need to figure out which other vehicles are coming with us in the morning. We should only take 4-wheel drive vehicles according to Charles. We're bringing my truck for hauling the horses. Charles said there is a campsite they used today where we can park that but they are moving their base camp out farther and he doesn't think a vehicle other than a 4-wheel drive can get there. Any suggestions?"

"Adele, Celeste and I all have 4-wheel drive Jeeps," Rose said. "I don't think Adele and Celeste ought to be out there in the desert all day in this heat. I can bring mine if that would help."

"Okay, that'll help. Maybe one of the other parents can spend the day with us. We can talk to them when they drop the girls off in the morning," he said. "It could be a long day. I think we should all hit the sack now and get some rest."

"Uncle Mike, I found Cutter's old halter and lead rope in your tack room. It's in the pile of stuff ready to go in the main barn," Brody said as he walked toward the back door. "Let's hope we find him so we can use it again."

CHAPTER | TWENTY-SEVEN

The detective in San Bernardino County got a call from a deputy in Yavapai County, Arizona around 8:00 a.m. on the third day after the four men left California with their horse and travel trailer. "I have some information for you," he said. "We have them in sight. I'm in the Prescott, Arizona office. We have a big rodeo in town this weekend. Four guys from Texas showed up a couple of days early and got paid to help set things up for this weekend. We found two trucks and two trailers that match the description on your bulletin. We haven't picked them up yet though. We have spotters on the rodeo grounds watching them. We'd like to take them all in one sweep, but we haven't been able to catch them all together in one place yet. Don't worry; they won't get out of here. If those guys are trying to hide, they picked the absolute wrong place to do it."

"Really?" the detective asked. "Why is that?"

"Put your coffee cup down first; I don't want you snorting coffee out your nose. I'm calling you from the Yavapai County Sheriff's Rodeo! The grounds are crawling with deputies, both on and off duty. Your clowns haven't seen the irony in that yet. But, I'm sure they will!"

"Oh, my goodness! I didn't see that coming!" the detective roared with laughter. "We have a big rodeo we sponsor here too, so I know what you mean about the deputies being everywhere. I think this case is in really good hands. Just so you know, if you hadn't heard, those four creeps stole a beautiful and very valuable AQHA stallion named Cut It Out. When they didn't get their ransom demand, they abandoned him without food, water or shelter in the middle of the desert out here. Just drove off and left him. We're scrambling to find him if we can. The owners and friends are also out in the desert looking for him."

"Oh, no!" the Arizona deputy said. "I know that horse. I've seen him in action, and so have several of my buddies. I'm going to let them know right away. Wish we were closer, we'd help you find him. But you don't have to worry about your four guys. They are never going to get away with this!"

"We're also working on a burner cell phone. Those four guys may have left it at the campsite where they kept their two hostages and the horse. If the battery on the phone holds out, we may be able to get a GPS location for it, so we know where to look. Hopefully, we'll get something back on that this morning. You keep an eye on our guys for us. We want 'em back in California as soon as we can get 'em here."

"You got it! Good luck on that cell phone thing. We got your back here in Arizona."

CHAPTER | TWENTY-EIGHT

At 4:15 a.m. the next morning, Hartley Ranch was a hive of activity. Mike had the 10-horse trailer hooked up earlier and drove it down to the main barn for loading. He'd asked two of his assistant trainers to come along on the search to help the girls out so they would be loading seven horses in the trailer. One of his assistants was in the process of filling the 100-gallon water tank in the trailer, and the other was loading the extra feed and equipment in the bed of the pick-up.

Mike waited with the gathering crowd on the back patio. Once everyone was there, he asked if there was another parent with a 4-wheel drive vehicle that could come with them for the day. He got one taker, Suzie's dad, Ryan. "Let me call my wife and let her know," was all he had to say.

Mike began dividing the group up into different vehicles. "I'm going to take Esteban and my two assistant trainers with me in the truck. Charles, you can take Brody, Maryann, and John. Rose can take Heidi, Melissa, and Kathy. Ginny will take Stevie, and the drone, the computer, and the radio equipment. Ryan, can you bring your daughter Suzy, and Rhonda. Before we head out, Charles was out there with John and the kids yesterday. They found a campsite that will work for me with the horse trailer and the horses. After we get that all offloaded, he will guide the other vehicles to a new campsite several miles closer to where they searched yesterday. The horses will have to walk to that. I'd like to divide the riders up into two separate groups. Skip will take Heidi and Suzy with him. Chet will take Melissa and Kathy with him. Becky, I would like you to split your time between the two groups. That way we can cover more ground. We're going to hand out radios to Maryann for the computer, Brody for the drone, me so I can keep in touch with all of you, Chet and Skip for the riders and leave one with Ginny and Becky. We'll give out others if needed. Rose put sets of ribbons together for the riders. You can mark your trail every quarter mile or so with ribbon so you can find your way back to camp. We're giving red ribbons to Chet and his group and green ribbons to Skip and his group. We don't need anyone else lost out there. Is everyone ready to go?"

The horses loaded in the trailer quickly. People stowed all backpacks and food items and other gear in vehicles. Those going climbed in for the drive. Charles led them because he knew where the first campsite was. They hit the road by 5:10 a.m. They reached the first turnoff at 6:20 a.m. and found the campsite for the horse trailer a few minutes later.

Everyone worked quickly and efficiently. The riders tacked the horses up and shouldered the backpacks and strapped helmets on. Brody led the horses on foot to the second campsite while the other vehicles followed Charles to it.

Once Charles' Jeep was parked, Maryann got out the laptop and turned it on. Brody took the drone out of its box and put the spare batteries in his backpack with his extra water bottles. He set the drone on the hood of Charles' Jeep and turned it on. One of the horses spooked at the sight but quickly calmed down until Brody used the controller and lifted it off the hood and got it flying. The horse spooked again a little, then settled down again. John found another set of footprints he and Rhonda left during their escape and pointed them out to the riders.

"This is what we are looking for on the ground. If you see these footprints, you are following our trail backward, and that will lead us to the mobile home and Cutter. If you guys on horseback find them, please give us a holler on the radio so we can get the drone to follow the trail. If you riders spread out and watch for those tracks on the ground, we'll probably get there sooner."

John radioed back to Mike that they were leaving and the search was beginning. Mike let Esteban hear the announcement. Tears formed in Esteban's eyes again. "I can't believe all these people are willing to give up their time to search for my boy. I can't thank them enough."

The mounted riders began at the point where John showed them the tracks they were looking for then spread out and slowly moved forward looking for more of them. Brody launched the drone and began moving it in a wide arc in front of the riders, looking for evidence of the trailer, corral, or any sign of habitation. Riders found tracks and followed them, then lost them again but continued moving forward. Brody saw nothing for hours.

****

Cutter nearly drained the water barrel on his second day of abandonment. There was not much left but sand in the bottom by 10 a.m. the third morning. Cutter licked it trying to absorb every ounce of water he could get out of it. His flanks were sunken, his tail hung on one end of his body, and his head hung on the other. His food ran out the first day. He was hungry. But the lack of water in the heat was more critical for him. He hadn't eaten well since the four men stole him from the Hacienda Rancho, but aside from losing some weight, he hadn't been in bad shape at all until the men drove off and left him there. He'd not seen anything but a few rabbits and a pack of coyotes since. He missed the companionship of his people. He was hungry. He was thirsty, and he was heartsick.

****

The day started out sunny and warm, but clouds began forming off to the west as a storm front moved in from the coast. They were scattered clouds at first. By 9:30 a.m. they began to billow up white and puffy on the top with grey bottoms. Winds blew them eastward across the desert. By 11:00 a.m., the clouds blocked the sun and turned dark as the wind increased in velocity. From a gentle breeze came a stiff wind about 10 to 15 miles per hour. It blew dust in front of it and wiped out most of the footprints John and Rhonda left in the desert soil during their escape.

Mike studied the clouds in the sky and began to worry. He'd not listened to the weather forecast for the day before leaving the ranch with this group of searchers. He fired up the engine in his big Dodge and turned on the radio, hoping to catch the weather forecast for the High Desert. He switched channels on the radio until he finally tuned in on a Los Angeles station with a weak signal. He could hear every other word, but even those were static-infused. He did hear a couple of words that gave him great concern. It sounded like they were predicting heavy rain in the Eastern desert area before nightfall. He wasn't sure or didn't hear exactly where they were predicting this rain.

Mike lived in the desert long enough to know about the monsoon rains that came up from Baja California or the southern Arizona desert during the summertime. The rain didn't last long, but it was heavy in spurts and caused flash flooding that could cause damage to property, roads, and other structures in its path. He had experienced storms that dropped over an inch of rain in 20 minutes time. Shallow washes became instant rivers with water flowing so fast it could push cars off roads, roll large rocks for hundreds of feet, and suck under any creature that happened to be in its path.

Mike continued studying the sky above him hoping there would be no sign of rain while the searchers were out here looking for Cutter. Clouds often formed, the wind blew, and the promise of rain never came to fruition. That was what created deserts in the first place. He decided to put everyone on notice anyway, just in case these clouds decided to dump on them. He called on the radio and suggested everyone stick to high ground as much as possible, especially if it did decide to rain.

The ones on horseback split up with Chet riding Duke, Melissa on Mighty Max and Kathy on Cricket heading out of the western side of the group. That left the eastern side to Skip riding Redd, Suzy on Dreamer, and Heidi on Schultzy. Becky and Prince Ali tried to keep in the middle as much as possible. The terrain was hilly in sections with steep washes from years of previous monsoon rains. She heard the call from Mike, as did Chet and Skip. Part of the trouble was the terrain. Chet could keep his eye on Melissa and Kathy better than Skip could. The western side of the search area had lower hills because the mountains created alluvial fans below their peaks. The lowest part of these alluvial fans was on the western side for many miles in the High Desert where they searched. Skip lost sight of Suzy and Heidi sometimes because they were climbing near the foot of the mountains and had deeper run-off areas carved out by millennia of monsoon storms. He, too, kept a watch on the sky above them. He was concerned about the weather. He knew nobody in the group was going to get hurt by a little rain. He knew about the raging torrents that could be the result of it though.

Suzy and Heidi, like Kathy and Melissa, were excited to take their horses out for a ride in a new area. They thought this would be a fun day for everyone. They certainly knew the consequences if they were unable to find Cutter but that was not their first motivation for going. They were normal teenaged kids. They thought they could do something good at the same time they were having some fun. They didn't expect what was about to happen.

CHAPTER | TWENTY-NINE

While the riders searched, Charles Carnegie left the camp spot in his Jeep looking for another way into the general area from the highway. He found one approximately five miles down the highway and radioed that information to the others. There was an easy road off the highway that he felt would also be good for Mike to bring the horse trailer to so the horses wouldn't have to backtrack so far at the end of the day. He took a couple of the colored ribbons and tied them to a stake near the highway so he and the others could find them before heading back to camp. Those on horseback and on foot in the desert were told about the relocation of the base camp with the GPS coordinates so they could use their cell phones to find it if needed. Mike put up a large American Flag on a pole attached to the horse trailer to increase their visibility to the others.

Close to noon, the searchers found the new base camp and stopped for a half an hour for lunch and to rest and water the horses. Mike, Chet, and Skip kept their eye on the sky hoping the storm would pass right on by them. The day was cooler because the clouds blocked the sun and the winds kept blowing which evaporated the sweat from humans and horses. The riders pulled the saddles and bridles off their horses so they could relax and dry off. They tied them to the trailer for their lunch with plenty of fresh water buckets before they ate their lunch. By that time everyone was keeping an eye on the clouds above them. They were getting darker and darker.

Forty-five minutes later, the riders tacked their horses up and began again with Brody and John setting off down the center on a northerly path. Chet's group searched the western side while Skip's group searched the eastern side upslope from the others. The footprints they looked for were gone. The wind from the brewing storm erased them. At that point, they were looking for any place they could find signs of habitation, specifically an old mobile home with a corral beside it. Brody and John looked for anything that might look familiar to John, any piece of old junk they may have passed in the night, any shape of rock that he may have seen, any wash they may have crossed. John walked ahead of Brody while he focused on keeping his drone in the air arcing from side to side to cover as much territory as possible.

The riders concentrated on small canyons that might hold the old mobile home. They climbed hills, down into arroyos and washes checking both sides of their trail. They spread out as far as they could and still be visible to others in their group. Becky and Ali took the point position in front of John and Brody, ranging west to east, staying within sight of the others as much as they could.

It was 1:30 p.m. that afternoon when Mike saw the first drop of rain hit the hood of his truck. It made a splat the size of a silver dollar on the dry hood and bounced a foot in the air before coming back down and sliding off the fender. Others followed it at intervals before it became a full-on downpour.

The raindrops were huge and pounded on the hoods and roofs of the vehicles and horse trailer. The sound was nearly deafening inside the vehicles. The windshield wipers couldn't keep up with the deluge. Visibility outside was cut short by the volume of water falling from the sky. The riders, Brody and John instantly soaked to the skin, halted their forward progress and stood still. Brody managed to get his drone down, landed it and picked it up. There was no sense trying to fly it in this.

The raindrops that hit the highest peaks began seeking lower ground and joining with other drops along the way. Trickles of water sought the lowest point and found their way into trenches made by previous rain storms. Small rivulets of water joined others and became small streams. Small streams joined others and became bigger streams. Bigger streams joined together and became rivers. The downhill velocity of the water increased exponentially.

This became Mike's nightmare. Flash flood! There were two people on foot and seven riders out in this unfamiliar territory. Mike spotted a muddy river heading in their direction and yelled at the other drivers to move their vehicles back ten feet. The channel the water followed was in front of the parked vehicles by several feet, but Mike knew those channels of water could change course at any time and erode their banks. He'd personally seen a car swept off a paved road into a ditch and he'd seen boulders weighing several tons pushed downstream by the force of the water. Once the vehicles all backed away from the stream bed, he got on the radio to the riders.

"Are you guys okay? Can you see the other riders? Remember to stay on high ground. If you are in a wash, get out of it now! You need to stay on the high ground!"

Brody radioed back that he and John were okay and he had the drone. Skip radioed in that he and Suzy and Heidi were standing just below a peak in the clear. He groused about being soaked to the skin. Chet radioed in that he had Becky with his group and they were clear at the moment.

That's when nature threw them another curve. Lightning streaked crackling across the sky and thunder boomed with deafening intensity. This was now Mike's worst nightmare! Lightning sought the highest points, and he had riders out there and people on foot as well that would be the highest points in their areas. All the people in the base camp could do was pray.

John knew the dangers, so he and Brody scrunched down close to the ground and huddled together during the onslaught. Brody did his best to keep the water out of the electronics on the drone and its controller so it would continue working when the rain stopped. He made an umbrella out of himself to do that.

Chet understood the dangers they faced. He had three young girls with him because Becky was closer to his group than Skips and joined them when the rain started in earnest. He dismounted and told the girls to do the same. Melissa's horse bolted at the first flash of lightning. Mighty Max screamed in terror as he ran. Melissa ran into the rain to catch him. Kathy's horse, Cricket, pulled the reins from her hand and followed the big pinto. Kathy ran to catch her horse as well. Prince Ali stood with Becky, head down and tail clamped to his butt with his butt turned to the wind. Chet didn't know whether to stay with Becky and Ali or chase the other two girls. Neither was a good choice since he and Becky were in a shallow draw at the moment. They watched as a small stream formed and began to trickle downhill a few feet in front of them. Chet had them move to higher ground for safety. They stood in the deluge halfway up a slight hill. They lost sight of Kathy and Melissa.

Skip looked for an overhang along the rocky wall of the peak he was on with Suzy and Heidi. He found a small one where a slab of limestone jutted out from the hill. It was only a few feet but gave the three riders some protection from the rain. They held onto their horses, but there wasn't enough room under the overhang for them too.

The torrential downpour continued for forty-five minutes with lightning crackling across the sky and thunderclaps deafening the searchers. Except for the ones at base camp who had access to shelter, the searchers got thoroughly drenched before the rain stopped. It didn't really stop, it slowed down, and the droplets got smaller and smaller until they ceased falling. The wind blew hard during the worst of the storm, driving the rain even harder. It stung the skin of those out in it, horses and humans alike.

The group on the western end of the search were the first ones in the clear. Chet and Becky looked around as the rain ceased pouring down. They couldn't go backward. There was a raging river of mud, sticks, entire Joshua trees and good sized rocks in the shallow draw they vacated during the storm. Becky couldn't believe how deep it was or how fast the water charged along its course. She'd never seen a flash flood up close.

Chet pulled out his radio and called for Mike. "Mike, we have a problem here. That first flash of lightning spooked two of our horses. They took off to the north. Before I could stop them, Kathy and Melissa ran after them. It's just Becky and Ali here with me now."

Mike's worst fears were hitting him. "Have you been able to spot them yet?" he asked Chet.

"No, the rain just stopped here. Becky and I will mount up and start looking. I'll let you know right away when we find them." Chet and Becky mounted their soggy horses and headed up the rise. Mighty Max was a large bay and white pinto. Chet hoped that would make him easier to find. He and Becky stood at the top of the rise and scanned the horizon. They saw nothing until they looked down. They did find hoofprints in the soggy ground. They began to follow them as Chet radioed in their intentions to Mike.

Mike shook his head as he walked to the group just getting out of their vehicles. "We've got a new wrinkle in our search today," he announced. He filled the group in on Chet's radio call. "Now we will have to search for the searchers as well as looking for Cutter."

"Oh, Dios mio, I'm so sorry," Esteban muttered. "All this trouble because of my horse. Now we must find three horses and two girls," he shook his head sadly.

CHAPTER | THIRTY

Becky found where horse prints of two horses overlapped each other. She pointed that out to Chet. "Looks like Mighty Max is leading and Cricket is following him. I see boot prints from Melissa and Kathy here too. I think we're on the right track." She told Chet.

The two riders followed the trail for quite a ways until they came to a wide wash at the bottom of an arroyo. Water raced through the channel it cut carrying sticks, debris, and rocks with it, crashing into the sides of the wash. The sound of crashing rocks, rushing water and debris made so much noise Chet and Becky had to shout at each other to be heard, and they were standing right next to one another. As Chet and Becky watched, whole sections of the far edge of the wash fell into the water. Chet looked down. His horse and Ali were standing close by the near edge of that same wash. As he looked, he saw a large crack form along the ground just barely in front of Ali's feet. "Get back!" he yelled at Becky as he pulled his horse backward. She pulled Ali's reins and sat back in the saddle. Ali stepped lightly back just in time. The whole edge of the wash they had been standing on fell into the whirling water below. Becky's heart pounded. That was too close!

"*Did you see that?*" Ali nickered to Duke.

"*Yeah, I did. I've seen this before. Do you remember the wash that runs beside the ranch back home? Well, I've seen that running full with six feet of water in it during one of these storms. If we don't stay away from the bank, you could get swept in and you'd be taking Becky with you. Stay away from the edges, okay,*" Duke explained.

"*You bet I will!*" Ali nickered back.

"Let's not get too close to the edge," Chet shouted to Becky. "Can you see tracks on the far side?"

Becky walked Ali along the wash but several feet from the edge for a way before she spotted something. She stopped and looked as closely as she could. "I think I see something over there," she pointed across the wash.

Chet joined her and searched the far bank. "Yes, I think you're right. That looks like a hoof print. Let's move downstream some and see if we can find a place to cross."

The two riders followed the stream west until it opened into a wide but shallow stream. "Do you think it's safe to cross here?" Becky asked looking across the expanse of water in front of her and Ali.

"Let me go first," Chet said as he slowly walked his horse into the stream. He sank in water up to the horse's pasterns. The water lost a lot of its velocity when it spread out across the plain. The desert soil began to absorb it as it slowed down. Chet picked his way across the stream and soon reached the other side. "You can follow my path. It's not too deep here," he called out to Becky.

Becky and Ali stepped into the water and made their way across. She and Chet changed directions and headed back to the last place they saw hoofprints and followed them. They didn't have to go far. They saw the two horses and girls cross over the top of a rise in front of them. The girls were on foot leading the horses. Becky trotted Ali to them. "You guys okay?" she asked them. Heidi was a muddy mess top to bottom and favored one leg a little.

"Yeah, we're good. We caught the horses and got back on to bring them back when another crack of thunder spooked them again. We held on and tried to stop them. Heidi took a fall, but she's not hurt bad. We finally got these poor babies under control and just stood with them until the thunder stopped," Melissa explained.

"They never heard thunder like that before," Heidi said. "It scared them to death!"

"Was that what that noise was?" Mighty Max asked Cricket. *"I thought something was coming to eat us whole in one bite."*

"Well, you certainly screamed like a mare!" Cricket chuckled under his breath. *"You ran like the hounds of Hades were on your heels."*

"Don't forget you were running for your life right with me!" retorted Max. *"And you were screaming like a little filly at the same time."*

"Okay, my friend. Let's just say we were both scared of the loud noise and leave it at that," chuffed Max. *"We need to help get our girls back to camp."*

"We found a place to cross a stream a little ways back. Do you think you can mount up and ride?" Chet asked Heidi and Melissa. "You need to get back to base camp and have someone look at that leg," he told Heidi. "Can you find your way back?"

"Yes, I can if the wind didn't blow the ribbons off the bushes. You guys should keep looking for Cutter. Maybe this rain is helping him. If those creeps left him a bucket or barrel, it should have rainwater in it now." Heidi said.

Chet handed his reins to Becky. "Hold this for me, will ya?" he said as he walked toward Heidi and Cricket. He gave her a boost up into the saddle while Melissa climbed back into hers. Chet mounted and led the way back to the stream he and Becky just crossed.

"Look at that!" Becky exclaimed when they reached the stream. The water was less than half as deep as it had been only a few minutes before. The parched desert soil was soaking the water up quickly.

Chet followed the tracks left by his horse and Ali back to where the other two horses spooked. He thought he could see the base camp from there and pointed it out to Heidi. "You be alright to ride back there by yourself?" he asked her.

"Oh, yes," she said. "Why don't you three go back and see if you can't find Cutter? I'll be fine." She turned her horse toward the base camp and set off at a slow trot.

Chet, Becky, and Melissa turned their horses around and continued the search. It was no longer possible for Becky to join Skip and his group. The washes higher up were still flowing strongly. She headed slightly east and north and continued searching while Chet and Melissa stayed a bit more to the west.

Skip, Suzie and Heidi had a more difficult time. As long as they stayed to the higher side, they could cross the many trickles they came across. They just couldn't move much lower without running into flooding streams for a while. They were all soaked to the skin, as were their horses, but they continued looking.

Redd groused about the water running into his ears. He hated that and there was nothing he could do about it. *"Darned* rain. *Makes it hard to hear sometimes,"* he said to Schultzy and Dreamer, shaking his head to clear his ears.

"I hate all this mud myself," Dreamer nickered. *"It is slippery and hard to get my balance on because it oozes out from under my shoes. I don't want to slip and fall and take Suzy with me."*

"Well, one thing that was not hard for any of us to hear were those thunder boomers," Schultzy muttered. *"They about scared the hair right off my hide. I wanted to run away but couldn't because we can't run down these hills with our riders. I've never heard them so loud before, have you?"*

Redd stopped shaking his head and looked thoughtful for a minute. *"Nope, I've never heard them this loud before. Sounded like they were right on top of us. But the lightning is what gets ya, ya know."*

"Really?" asked Dreamer. *"I thought it was just bright light that hurt your eyes."*

"When I was a youngster in Texas, before I came to the ranch, I saw a bolt of lightning come out of the sky and hit a young steer in the next field over from us horses. That steer dropped like a rock. His legs twitched once or twice. I think the humans call it dying. The life left it, just like that. I saw smoke come off that poor steer and it never moved again. That was more frightning to me than the loud noise of the thunder," Redd explained. *"I ran to my mother and huddled next to her in fear."*

"Oh, my goodness. That would make me afraid of lightning too," Schultzy nickered. *"I will never look at lightning the same way again. I'd rather be inside in my nice safe barn stall than outside when lightning and thunder comes."*

"Just be glad you have a nice safe barn stall to be in when the storms like this come," Redd suggested. *"It makes you appreciate your owner a lot more."*

Schultzy and Dreamer thought about what Redd said. His comments convinced them they had to take care of Heidi and Suzy. They were good owners who looked after them well and loved them. They would be very careful while Heidi and Suzy rode them.

The search continued on the upslope. There were no footprints to find, so they began looking for any sign of habitation. They did find several old mine shafts on the upper slopes which Skip urged the girls to avoid. They also saw the rubble left from a couple of old cabins originally made of wood which had fallen in on themselves. There was generally a debris field around them of old pieces of metal, rusted out tin cans and the like. Over the next hour, the rushing water reduced to trickles everywhere and was no longer a threat.

Brody and John dried off the drone. Brody replaced the batteries and resumed flying it. They saw more destruction from the flooding than anything else.

Becky climbed a slight hill and stopped Ali. She sat there looking around when she thought she heard something. Ali heard it too. He recognized it as the snort of another horse. He lifted his head and blared out his stallion challenge in the direction he thought the snort came from.

Becky was startled, then startled again when something answered Ali's call. She rode Ali down a slight incline to another hill a bit higher than the one they had stopped on. When they reached the top, around the edge of another slight hill she thought she could see part of the roof of a house. Could it be the mobile home? She crossed her fingers and toes but stopped long enough to radio it in to the other searchers. She stayed at the top of the hill so others could see her, including Brody with his drone. The drone flew above her very quickly.

As soon as she heard from Chet and Brody, she walked down the other side of the hill into a tight little arroyo, surrounded on three sides by hills. In the bottom center of that arroyo sat an older mobile home that looked abandoned. She saw no cars or trucks around, but there was some trash blowing in the wind that appeared newer and a few shiny cans in the late afternoon light. She crossed her fingers again and walked around the end of the mobile home. She walked past a window standing open. The breeze blew an old curtain outside the mobile home. If someone left that window open decades ago, the wind would have long since shredded the curtain, but it wasn't. It was wet from the rain. Could this be the place? She remembered Maryann's explanation of how John and Rhonda got away and her heart was tripping in her chest. When Becky and Ali reached the other side of the mobile home, she saw the makeshift corral with a miserable looking horse standing in the middle of a lake inside it. He was a palomino.

Prince Ali nickered to the horse. He nickered back and dropped his head again. Becky noticed he didn't look well, he was sunken in at the flanks and looked about ready to drop. She got on her radio. "We found him!" She jumped off Ali and pulled the three water bottles she had stashed in her saddlebag out, rushed to Cutter's corral and dumped them into his water bucket.

Those three 16 ounce bottles didn't do much to slake Cutter's thirst, but they helped him revive a little. He suddenly recognized the fact that another stallion was standing outside his stall. He screamed his stallion challenge at Prince Ali.

Ali shook his head. *"Hey, Cutter. I'm not here to take you on. I'm here to find your raggedy butt and get you back to civilization. Don't threaten me, please."*

Cutter stared at Ali, taken aback by his comments. *"I'm sorry. I apologize. That was a first instinct. It won't happen again. I am sure glad to see you two. Can you get me back home?"*

"That's what we're here for buddy," Ali said to him. *"Just hang in there. The people are going to try and find the road in here with the trailer so we can get you out."*

"Oh, thank you! Thank you for coming for me. I thought I would die alone out here until you showed up," Cutter muttered softly.

Becky was on the radio to Brody and Mike. "We need to get him some water. I only had three bottles with me and they're already gone. I don't think he got much out of that storm. There's a trace in the bottom of his bucket, but it was mostly mud. He's pretty sucked up in the flank. I'm going to wait here with him."

CHAPTER | THIRTY-ONE

Chet and Melissa came over the rise a few minutes later. They dumped the water bottles they carried with them into Cutter's bucket as well. It was all gone in a minute or two. The three of them looked Cutter over. He had no cuts or scratches on his body they could see. He appeared to have lost weight during his ordeal, and he was desperately thirsty. They talked among themselves as they waited for the others to join them.

Brody confirmed with Maryann the drone had shown her good GPS coordinates for the mobile home. He couldn't see the pictures from his location, but Maryann could. Stevie sat beside her in Grandpa's Jeep watching the laptop monitor and he was bouncing up and down. She was shaking with excitement when she saw Cutter standing in the corral beside the mobile home. Brody and John sprinted back to the base camp.

Mike's cell phone rang. It was the San Bernardino County detective calling him. "We did get a location on that cell phone the guys used for their ransom demand. It's way out in the desert. We pinged it and got a GPS location for it. I've got deputies on their way to that location now. They're going to meet with the Kern County Deputies."

"We think we found the location ourselves," Mike told him. "We've been out here since daybreak and found the horse a couple of minutes ago. He's alive but not in great shape. We are going to get our vehicles back on the highway so we can find the road in."

"Why don't I have my deputies meet you at the highway. The Kern County deputies think they know which turnoff to use. You can drive in with them. That way you can get the horse out of there without disturbing the scene. We've sent in our people so they can photograph and fingerprint the trailer and gather any evidence left there."

"Great! We'll wait at the highway for your deputies. You can let them know we have a truck and ten-horse trailer plus a couple of other 4-wheel drive vehicles. We'll be waiting beside the highway for them. You got an E.T.A. for them by chance? We're sort of in a hurry. The horse needs water badly. We have it with us. We have a couple of riders at the corral with the horse right now, but their 16-ounce water bottles are not going very far. Just in case, if your guys get up the highway, tell them to look for the red and green ribbons on the south post of the dirt road going back into the desert bike area. We're on our way now." Mike disconnected his phone.

"Charles, Rose, Ginny and Ryan, we need to get moving! Deputies from San Bernardino County and Kern County will meet us alongside the highway. The Kern County guys think they know the turnoff we need. Chet and Melissa are there already with Becky. We're loading the rest of the horses now."

Rose and Ginny quickly finished washing out the scrapes on Heidi's leg. "We can put band-aids on this when we get there if you're okay now," Ginny told her. Rose gently smoothed in an antibiotic cream on the wound.

"I'll be fine," Heidi said. "I wish I was with them when they found Cutter. That must have been exciting to see."

Esteban was nearly in tears again. "Do you think he's going to be okay?" he asked Mike.

"Yeah, I'm sure of it. Chet and Becky say he's still standing. That's a good sign. Chet thinks he'll be fine with some feed and water. They have a little water with them. That should help until we get there. Hang in there, my friend. We're going to get your horse out of there safe and alive."

Mike, Rose, Ginny, Ryan, and Charles all arrived at the exit point and parked alongside the highway. They didn't have to wait long. The first to arrive were two cars from the Kern County Sheriff's Office. They turned around on the highway and pulled in line in front of Mike's truck. Two SUV's from San Bernardino County got in line a few minutes later. The deputies and Mike spoke for a minute beside the road. "We're only about six miles from the turnoff that will get us to that mobile home. If you didn't know where the turnoff was, you'd miss it. You can't see the mobile home from the road. We know right where it is. Follow us. We'll get you there. It's going to be a very sharp turn to the right, more than 90 degrees. Watch that turn with your trailer," one of the deputies told him.

Everyone got back in their vehicles and pulled out onto the highway following the Kern County deputy. Six miles later when Mike pulled off the road following the deputy, he saw what the man meant. He would never have seen that turnoff. It curved downward and then to the south before following the contours of the land into a small canyon surrounded on three sides by baren rocky hills.

Mike pulled up to the mobile home behind the squad cars and stopped. Esteban hopped out of the truck immediately and dashed around the mobile home looking for the corral and his horse. He stumbled and whirled his arms around to regain his footing and kept running. He ignored everything else until he finally saw Cutter in the makeshift corral. He rushed toward his horse like a man possessed. He climbed over the corral and jumped down into it, talking in a soothing voice to his horse. He threw his arms around his neck and hugged him like a long-lost friend. He sobbed with joy and relief. "Oh, my boy. I'm so glad to see you. What have they done to you? We'll get you better. You'll see!" Then he lapsed into his melodic first language, Spanish. Neither of them seemed to mind the mud.

Mike grinned. "What do you know, we have us a bi-lingual horse here." Cutter had his head across Esteban's shoulder with his eyes half closed, enjoying the attention of his best friend.

The people with the search party grabbed buckets and began filling them from the tank in the trailer. They hauled buckets to the corral and dumped them into the half barrel that had been used for Cutter's water supply by the men who stole him. Esteban walked Cutter to the barrel to let him drink. He drank and drank and drank as the water buckets kept coming. He finally slaked his thirst enough to push his soggy muzzle into Esteban's chest.

Mike walked around the corral, looking it over. It was a patchwork of pieces of old lumber nailed together with no gate at all. "We're going to have to dismantle part of this to get Cutter out of there," he finally told the group. "Those clowns never intended him to get out of this. I didn't bring any tools with us except for my small toolbox in the trailer. I think I only have one hammer. The screwdrivers and pliers won't help us much with this project. And they used lots of nails. It's a wonder Cutter didn't cut himself up with the way they put those in. Oh, and we're going to get muddy."

One of the deputies came outside of the mobile home shaking his head, "We found the phone and the handcuffs in there. This place must have been rustic living at its finest. How is the horse? Is he going to be okay?"

Ginny was walking back from the corral when the deputy stepped out. She looked at him and smiled, "Yes, he's going to be fine in a few days. He's gone without proper food for a while, and he was out of water for a day or so, but he'll recover. He's going to be okay," she nodded her head. She went to the trailer and picked up Cutter's halter and lead rope. She walked it back to the corral and handed it over the fence to Esteban.

"Esteban, can you put this on him and hold him to one side of the corral. Mike and the guys are going to have to break the corral down," she told him. "I'll have Brody bring him some hay to keep him busy. Keep him as calm as you can. The guys are going to have to haul the wood away so he doesn't step on any nails getting out of there."

One of the girls came over with apples in her hand and gave them to Esteban for Cutter. Brody brought a small flake of hay and handed it to Esteban. Because the ground was soggy inside the corral, Estaban splayed his hands out like a plate to serve Cutter. Cutter was most interested in the apples and polished them off with Esteban's help then ripped into the hay with relish. Ginny laughed, "Looks like Cutter is going to get a lot of babying for a while!"

Mike, John, Chet, and Skip climbed over the rail and jumped in the corral. It was small so it became fairly crowded. The corral was cobbled together of old lumber. Some of it was nearly rotten. The men began kicking at it with their boots. It took some effort, but they were finally able to kick out one side of the corral. The kids pulled pieces of wood off as they split and tossed them in a pile to one side. When the last piece finally came down, Brody and Stevie pulled the section away. It left a large space so Esteban could walk Cutter through without worrying about scratching his sides or stepping on nails. Cutter was finally free!

When Esteban Garcia walked his beloved Cutter out of the corral, the entire group clapped and cheered! Everyone was smiling. Everyone was happy they were there to see that. Those who spent the day in the desert searching for the horse was relieved he was alive and able to walk out on his own. They celebrated by eating and drinking most of the food and drinks they'd brought along, chatting among themselves, remembering high points during the search and things they'd seen along the way. They talked a lot about the storm that blew in and the havoc it caused. Heidi had help to put the band-aids on her scrapes. She told the others they caught their two missing horses and decided to ride them back. One big thunder boomer went off directly over their heads and Cricket zigged while Heidi zagged. She fell off. It wasn't something Cricket caused. She slipped because her saddle was wet. The group celebrated Brody for his ability to keep his drone up and show them the way. They celebrated Prince Ali for being the first to hear Cutter. Maryann was celebrated for the idea to search in the first place. Esteban Garcia was on top of the world because his horse was found alive!

When they polished off the last sandwich, and the last of the cookies, fruit and crackers were a memory, the saddles and bridles were pulled off the horses and stowed. They organized the disarray of equipment and put it all away in the vehicles. They loaded the horses in the horse trailer and made sure the hay nets were full. The group piled in for the long drive back to Hartley Ranch.

CHAPTER | THIRTY-TWO

Becky's mom, Caroline Howard, decided to stay in the High Desert with Maryann's Aunt Adele and Uncle Roy rather than driving an empty horse trailer home and returning to pick it up again the next day. Becky called her when they found Cutter. Caroline let Adele and Roy know. Celeste Carnegie also got a call from Charles with the good news. He told Celeste about the logistics of getting everyone back to the ranch so she figured out how much time they had and called Adele. The women took Roy and went shopping. When they arrived at Hartley Ranch with their bundles of groceries, Caroline found the back door key in its hiding place, and the women invaded Ginny's kitchen once more.

Kathy, Heidi, and Melissa called their parents about finding the horse. Ryan, Suzy's dad, called his wife. Word began to circulate. Families of the young people involved came to the ranch to meet the famous stallion and his owner. They were pressed into service setting the patio up for a celebration or helping in the kitchen. Someone called the local newspaper to let them know the famous Prince Ali was involved. Ali was the first to hear the missing horse and lead his owner, Becky

Howard, right to him. The reporter, looking to boost his career, searched the internet and found articles about Cut It Out. He realized that Cutter was a valuable horse in his own right. He called several buddies. The press began swooping down on the incident. Print reporters showed up at the ranch while the TV news crews drove up from the Los Angeles basin.

Roy tended the grill and put on tri-tip roasts while he set up the cold drink station with buckets of ice filled with bottled water, soft drinks and iced tea.

Mike pulled into his driveway leading the caravan of 4-wheel drive vehicles and saw the ranch filling with family members. Then he noticed the news people. He slumped his shoulders and let out a great sigh as he drove the trailer to the front of the main barn for unloading. The news people quickly made their way to the barn to get their story. Mike thought he might as well put up a news office next to the barn for them. They'd already been there twice this year. The first time was when they identified Prince Ali as the stray horse that wandered onto their ranch. The second time was when the kids returned from Colorado after being caught in front of the second largest wildfire in Colorado history. And here they were again!

Mike parked the truck, shut off the engine and set the brake before stepping out. The young people and his assistant trainers opened the rear door of the horse trailer and began pulling horses out. Reporters shouted questions at the young people. Mike stepped up and said, "Can you please wait until we get all the horses off the trailer. I don't want to see any of the horses or these young people hurt. Let them do what they need to do; then you are free to ask questions if you don't mind."

Esteban Garcia handled Cutter himself, walking the horse to a freshly bedded stall with hay in the feeder. Cutter immediately dropped down and rolled in the bedding. It felt good for him to be back inside a normal stall with a roof, fresh water, food, and a soft place to lay down.

The youngsters pulled their horses out and put them in stalls while they unpacked the balance of the gear and the tack taken for the search. As soon as they finished unloading the trailer, Mike drove it back to the trailer parking area and dropped it off the truck and parked his truck. He walked down to the barn. Reporters were trying to ask questions of the girls while they rinsed their horses off. Kathy squirted Melissa, and the water fight behind the barn was on. Everyone who'd been in the desert searching for Cutter was sweaty and dirty and covered in desert dust and mud. The water from the hoses was so refreshing; they shared it with each other as they rinsed their horses off, including Chet and Skip. The whole bunch of them were dripping wet in minutes once again. They finished rinsing the horses, sweat scraped them off and put them on the hot walkers to dry while they laughed and joked with each other.

The reporters took some great photos of the water fight and kept themselves far enough away from the action to stay reasonably dry. While the horses walked on the hot walkers, the girls took to the benches that lined the inside of the barn aisle. The reporters asked them questions about their participation in the search for Cut It Out.

Esteban Garcia stood at the door to Cutter's stall watching his horse while the girls pulled theirs out to rinse them off. Cutter didn't seem to want to get up once he sprawled in the bedding. Esteban walked back into the stall and scrunched himself down in the bedding and picked Cutter's head up and laid it across his lap. He sat there talking softly to his horse, stroking his cheek and neck. Cutter exhaled something like a snort and closed his eyes, enjoying the attention from his "heart human."

A photographer opened the stall door wide enough to get his lens inside the stall and snapped a photo of the man with his horse. The flash startled Cutter. His eyes opened. He lifted his head off Esteban lap. Esteban reassured him and continued stroking his neck. He looked at the photographer and asked "Can you please give me a few minutes with my boy? I'll come out and talk to you in a little while. He's tired. He's been through an ordeal. I'd like him to rest."

The photographer backed away from the stall and mentioned the conversation to his colleagues who agreeably left Mr. Garcia and his horse alone. The TV reporters arrived with their cameramen and talked to the young people involved in the search efforts under Mike Hartley's supervision.

Cutter lay with his head in Esteban's lap for a few more minutes before he decided he was hungry and stood up to eat. Esteban scratched his withers on his way out of the stall and went looking for the photographer he'd spoken to. "I'm available now. My horse is having his dinner at the moment. What can I tell you?"

The print and TV reporters stood around Esteban Garcia and Mike Hartley outside the barn for better lighting and asked their questions. Mike explained he had trained the horse for Mr. Garcia years before and attended cutting competitions across the country with Cutter. They both had a loving relationship with the horse and were appalled when someone stole him. Mr. Garcia explained how he found out about the situation only after John and Rhonda Powell made their escape. He was in Spain because of his mother-in-law's illness. Mike brought the reporters up to date with the details of the search for Cutter and their successful conclusion late that afternoon. He said their veterinarian was due shortly to check the horse over for any health issues, but he appeared to be in good shape. Mr. Garcia went into Cutter's stall and haltered him and walked him out so the reporters could take a look at him and any photographs they wanted, then put him back to finish his dinner. Satisfied, the reporters all left the property and dinner on the patio began.

That evening, the families and friends all celebrated! Everyone, including Esteban Garcia, was in high spirits. The kids who rode in the search party enjoyed the water fight in the barn. It washed off some of the mud and desert dust and cooled them down. Brody and Maryann took part because it was fun. They all sat around the patio in damp jeans and tee-shirts, but it felt good.

The festivities were short-lived because those who'd spent their day searching the desert for Cutter were tired. Esteban ate his meal and nearly fell asleep over it. He'd not had enough sleep since he left Spain with Stevie. Mike and Ginny suggested he stay the night again and Ginny walked him to her guest room. Stevie and Brody talked over dinner and decided Stevie would get the top bunk tonight, but they wanted to play a few games first. When the other families left for home, John and Rhonda left for the Hacienda Rancho. Carolyn Howard decided to stay one more night with Rose Wilcox. She and Becky could take Prince Ali home the next morning after everyone had a good night's sleep. The group slowly left until Mike and Ginny were the only ones left on the patio.

Mike looked at his wife and told her, "I'm tired myself. I wasn't out riding in that heat or that gully washer today, but I was on the radio constantly with those who were. I can't believe how great the young people reacted to this and how they pitched in to help. Even Susie, your problem child, was out there busting her chops to find a horse she'd never seen before. Actually, out of that group, Brody is the only one who ever had. Maryann and her drone idea was a streak of genius! And Brody took it and ran with the idea. I'm so proud of those kids! If you don't mind, I think I will talk to Esteban tomorrow about Desert Rose. It's time for Brody to have his very own horse. What do you think?"

"I think it was time for him to have his very own horse a long time ago," Ginny said. "It wouldn't take us much time to get Rosie ready for competition. Then Brody can join his friends."

"You think he wants to do that?" Mike asked.

"You should have seen him at the Youth National Championship show. He was hanging around the rail watching everyone else compete and busting his fanny to help them get ready. I think he wanted to join them but didn't want to say anything. He's as good a rider as any of the kids Chris and I took to that show. With a horse like Rosie, he'll be in the winner's circle with them instead of just watching them from the sidelines. I'd love to see that happen for him."

CHAPTER | THIRTY-THREE

Several hours later, Ginny got up from bed and went to the kitchen for a glass of water. She noticed Brody's bedroom door was open as she passed it and she expected to meet him in the kitchen fixing himself something to eat. Boys his age just couldn't be filled up. They were always hungry. When she turned the kitchen light on, she was surprised Brody wasn't digging around in the refrigerator. He wasn't in the kitchen at all. She got her glass of water and checked the living room and the den and didn't see him. She poked her head out the back door and saw the light on in the barn.

Ginny went back to her bedroom and pulled on her bathrobe and slippers. She walked down to the barn quietly so she did not disturb other horses. When she stepped in the barn, Clyde was laying on the mats in front of Rosie's stall and wagged his tail at her, banging the mat with it in the process. That alerted Brody. "What is it boy?" he asked Clyde stepping out of Rosie's stall.

"Just me," Ginny said, "I was wondering who was in the barn at 1:00 in the morning."

"I didn't mean to wake anyone. I just wanted to spend some time with Rosie before she goes home tomorrow. I heard John and Rhonda telling Mr. Garcia they'll come back and bring their trailer to haul the horses home."

Ginny didn't want to give away her conversation with Mike. "John and Rhonda won't be here until late morning or early afternoon. You have plenty of time with Rosie. Why don't you get some sleep? I'd bet you are pretty tired right now."

"Okay, I'll be back inside in a minute. I'll shut off the lights," Brody told her. His heart sank. He expected Mr. Garcia to take his horses back to his ranch, but he'd hoped they would be there another day or two. He just confirmed his Rosie would be gone sometime in the morning. He was heartbroken all over again. He didn't want to say anything to anyone about it. He wandered back to bed and lay on his bed trying to come up with ways to keep Rosie. He only had a few dollars in his pocket, a piggy bank more full of copper pennies than silver, and his personal savings account had $606.00 in it. He'd been saving for a car when he was old enough to drive. In his mind, black and white images began to filter into his consciousness. His first images were Rosie as a newborn. She was a chestnut baby with a fine thick coat because of the temperatures at that early time of year. She had the face of an Arabian horse with a jibah, the bulge of her forehead above her eyes, large dark eyes set wide on her face, and a fine muzzle. Her neck was long and curved. Her loin was long and level, and she had legs for days. Her legs had beige hair from the knee down to the white markings. Her tiny hooves were white because the dark hair didn't meet the coronet band at her hooves. She was refined and elegant, but she was as sassy as the devil. She was independent, even then. She went to her mother when she was hungry, but drifted off to do her own exploration of her environment when she was satisfied. She loved to explore every rock, every rail in her turn out, everything that drifted into her environment. She studied the desert ravens who landed on the rails of the turnout. She watched the sparrows who settled in the trees around it. She watched the mice who attempted to live off spilled grain tossed into feeders. She was curious about everything. And she learned who was a friend and who might be a foe very quickly.

One individual caught her attention right off. It was Brody. He came to visit her every day after school and first thing in the mornings on the weekends. He had the most wonderful scratches for her withers. He brushed her coat while it was shedding out for the summer time. He had magic fingers that knew just where she itched.

Brody saw it all. He watched her in the arena for the first time when she finally got to stretch her legs and run. He saw her crash into the rails while she figured out how far back she needed to put on her brakes. He saw when her mother rejected her for banging her head on her milk bag. She walked away dejected. He was there to comfort her. He offered her his two fingers to suck on. At first, she had milk teeth that had no bite. But as she grew, he had to teach her to suck, not bite. He taught her how to lead by haltering her and letting her follow her mother back to their stall. They got used to each other and their schedules. She knew when he came home from school and was waiting for him, nickering for attention.

He was the one who discovered her in the turnout with the calf that got loose and called his uncle over to watch her. That's when Uncle Mike learned she was a natural born cow horse. He watched Uncle Mike begin her training with the groundwork he always did with young horses. He saw her learn how to stop on command, how to lead, and how to turn.

He watched with great interest when Uncle Mike bitted her up for the first time and began teaching her how to ground drive with the long lines. Uncle Mike taught her how to stop, how to turn left or right and how fast he wanted her to go by walking beside or behind her with the long lines through a training surcingle. He used a soft, padded baby bit on her as they worked. He watched and absorbed the lesson himself so he could teach it to another youngster someday. He was just more interested because it was Rosie getting the lesson.

Brody was standing at the rail the first time Uncle Mike got on her back. She never flinched. She moved out the way he directed her as if she'd been doing it for years. They only walked and did a bit of jogging the first time. It wasn't until Uncle Mike was confident in her that he asked her for the lope. She was comfortable with it, and so was he. He remembered how proud he was of her as he watched Uncle Mike put her through her paces. He tried to figure out how he was going to ride her himself.

That came up a few weeks later. Mike had a habit of taking his young training horses off the property for short trail rides when they were far enough along in their training to do so. Sometimes he rode them himself and sometimes Brody or one of his assistant trainers did that in a group of two or three horses. Brody offered. Mike let him ride the first time Rosie left the arena for a ride on the trails. It was the most wonderful ride. Rosie was curious and somewhat cautious of strange things she saw on the trail, but not overly so. She was steady and careful, and she trusted Brody. He could hardly wait to ride her again. It gave him an opportunity to be with her and ride her. Afterward, he got to spend extra time with her when he groomed her.

Rosie became his "go to girl" when it came to trail riding. Uncle Mike asked him about that. "She's so calm I don't have to think about it. That way I can enjoy the ride without worrying about a horse going off over a piece of paper blowing across the trail in front of us." Mike knew that was true and his client's horse was getting the experience she needed, so he thought no more about it.

When Rosie was a little older, Mike finally tried her on a handful of his calves to see how she reacted. Chet and Skip were mounted in the arena as turn-back riders when Mike took Rosie in. She stopped in the center of the arena and just looked at the cows, watching their every move. Mike asked her to walk among the cows. She picked her target and moved the calf away from the others. That calf's single-minded goal was to get back in the herd with his buddies. Rosie went to work. Brody watched from the rail. Rosie nearly sat down on her butt and hocks to keep her front end moving to block that calf. She was as quick as lightning, and she was effective. Mike had to hang onto the saddle horn to stay seated. She got low enough his boot heels dragged the dirt several times. She moved quicker than the cow when he took off in another direction. She held that calf longer than the required time for competition. Mike had to take her out of the arena to get her to relax and leave it go.

Rosie was a sweaty mess, but the activity exhilarated her. She loved it! She wanted to do it again and jigged all the way to the barn. Uncle Mike smiled broadly as he dismounted and put her in the cross ties. "I think we have another Cutter on our hands. I need to teach her when to stop though. This mare will work the pounds off those calves if I let her."

Brody laughed. "Guess we'd better feed her up too. She really works it out there! I've never seen another horse so much like Cutter. She could be your next champion."

Within a few weeks, she entered the arena with the cows calmly and walked through the herd, made her selection and kept that calf away from his buddies for the right amount of time and relaxed when Uncle Mike picked the reins back up and walked her away.

Mike's only problem with Rosie was her size and her looks. Cutter was a 1,200-pound animal people usually saw in the cutting arena. Rosie was a delicate 900-pound horse that looked more like an Arabian than a Quarter Horse. She was pretty and her tail flagged when she was getting down on her cow. She didn't look the part at all. She was all cowgirl in behavior but looked more like a princess. He wasn't quite sure what to do with her.

When Uncle Mike was busy with another horse, Brody started working Rosie in the reining patterns. He didn't put her in the sliding stop but worked the riding in circles at different speeds. He added the change of direction with flying lead changes in the middle of the arena to work in the opposite direction. Her first few times were clumsy at the transitions in speed and direction changes, but he kept at it with her until her circles were perfectly round and her change of direction was effortless.

Brody used the tractor to groom one of the secondary arenas one morning and asked Uncle Mike to watch. With no hoofprints in the arena, the patterns would be more clear to Uncle Mike. Brody rode Rosie in and put her through the reining pattern used at the big shows except for the sliding stops. He had Uncle Mike look at the hoofprints so he could see clearly how round her circles were and how smooth her transitions were even on the ground.

"I think Esteban will be very pleased. This little mare is such a good cutting horse, and I think she's going to make a great reining horse as well. Let's get her fitted with protective sport boots and teach her how to slide!"

Brody could have popped the buttons off his shirt right then but kept his feelings to himself. He'd been very careful not to show any more affection for Rosie than he did to the other horses he got to work with under Uncle Mike's tutelage. He reserved that for times in the barn when he was alone with Rosie. She still squealed her baby squeals on occasion with him. When she was nervous or upset, he let her suck on his fingers for a few minutes to calm down. He loved her to distraction, and she loved and trusted him. That was why he was so devastated when he came home from school and found her gone. He was not prepared for that and didn't have time to say goodbye to her. He sucked it up and pretended it did not affect him. The only time he didn't was late at night in the quiet of his bedroom, and he was careful about that too.

Tomorrow was going to be another long day. He tried to shut down his mind as the memories kept coming. He didn't drift into sleep until the rosy glow of morning began creeping over the desert from the east.

CHAPTER | THIRTY-FOUR

Stevie woke up to the smell of freshly brewed coffee and blueberry pancakes. He scuttled off the top bunk and headed for the kitchen. He usually had a cup of coffee with his parents so he asked Ginny if he could have one. He glanced over and noticed his dad was already sitting at the kitchen table having a cup of his own. Ginny nodded as she flipped two more pancakes on the grill and removed two others to the oven to keep warm. "Did you sleep well Stevie?" she asked him.

Stevie yawned and stretched his arms wide, "Yes, Mrs. Hartley. I did. I think I've about caught up now."

"Is Brody up yet?" she asked him.

"Brody wasn't in the bedroom when I got up. I assumed he was out here having breakfast with you," Stevie said.

Ginny smiled to herself and nodded. "He's probably out in the barn again then."

"Does he go to work with Mike this early?" Stevie asked her.

"Not usually," Ginny said. "He's probably down in the barn with Rosie. I found him down there at 1:00 this morning."

"Is there something wrong with my horse?" Esteban asked concerned.

"No, she's doing fine. She needs to gain back a few pounds, but Doc Martin said she'd be right as rain in a week."

"Is there something I should know then?" Esteban asked her.

"Mike should be back up here for breakfast in a few minutes. We can talk about it then. How many pancakes would you like? How many would you like, Stevie?"

"I'd like three of them to start, Mrs. Hartley. They smell wonderful," Stevie said as he took another sip of his coffee and stared across the table at his father with a question mark on his face.

Mike walked in the back door and pulled his work boots off. He walked into the kitchen in stocking feet. "That smells wonderful. Can a cowboy get a plate of those?" he said to his wife.

"Sure, when you get your hands washed up," she told him laughing. "I'm going to fix some for Esteban. Yours are next."

"Okay, Mike's here, so what's the deal with Rosie and Brody?" Esteban asked again.

Mike poured himself a cup of coffee and walked to the kitchen table. "It's something we didn't know anything about until we picked the horses up at your ranch a few days ago. Rosie about knocked me on my butt and pulled the lead rope out of my hand to get to Brody when she first saw him. We were shocked. She sounded like a baby horse. She went a little crazy. I've never seen anything like it before. Brody couldn't keep his hands off her either."

"It seems they had a very close relationship we knew nothing about," Ginny explained. "We had no idea how Brody feels about Rosie, or how Rosie feels about Brody either for that matter until she came back here. It was a surprise to us. We would have talked to you about Rosie before you took her home if we had known."

Esteban sat thinking. "This is something I would like to see for myself. We'll talk about it again later." He picked up his fork and dived into Ginny's blueberry pancakes, savoring every bite. Stevie and Mike dove into theirs as well, soaking up all the syrup with the last bite of pancake. Ginny finished up the batch and had time to enjoy a couple of them herself after she put a few in foil in the warming oven for Brody if he ever got back to the house.

Esteban and Mike had another cup of coffee when they polished off their plates before Esteban suggested, "Let's get down to the barn and check on my handsome boy." The two men got up from the table and walked out. Stevie began picking up dirty plates and cutlery from the table while Ginny ate the last bite of her breakfast.

"Stevie, you don't have to do that," she said. "I'll get the dishes done in a minute."

"No, Mrs. Hartley. I help my mother with the dishes every meal. I don't mind, really."

Ginny smiled at him. "You wouldn't want to move in here would you?" she asked laughing. "There are days I could use the help."

"If you guaranteed blueberry pancakes for breakfast every day, I'd see what I can do," Stevie laughed back. He rinsed the dishes and helped stack them in the dishwasher for Ginny. He then washed her cast iron skillet out with hot water only and dried it carefully with paper towels so it didn't rust. His mother taught him well. Ginny was impressed. "Are you sure you don't want to move in here?" She laughed again as they put things away and Ginny started the dishwasher. "Why don't you head for the barn and see what the menfolk are up to?" she suggested.

Esteban and Mike walked into the barn. Brody was nearly done grooming Rosie in the barn aisle. He'd bathed her, clipped her, and braided her mane and tail. She was all over Brody with her nose, pushing him as he walked around her, and grabbing at his clothes as he worked at her side. She nickered or squealed at him continuously, but stood perfectly still as he braided her mane. He talked to her nonstop while he worked on her, kidding her, poking fun at her, and joking with her as though she understood his language. And she did. She understood the language of Brody perfectly. He expressed his affection for her in every stroke of the brush he pressed against her skin. And he understood her language just as well. Every nicker, every squeal, every tug for attention was clear. These two were an item! Had they been a "boy/ girl combination" Uncle Mike would have called Brody aside to explain the facts of life to him. He and Esteban stood quietly and watched while Brody and Rosie were unaware they had company.

Brody suddenly turned toward the front of the barn and saw Mike and Esteban. His face turned red. He stuttered, " Oh, ah, hi there, I didn't know there was anybody here. Did you need me for something Uncle Mike? I was grooming Rosie, and I thought I'd groom her mother before John and Rhonda take them home. Chet and Skip are grooming the others so they'll be ready to get home too."

Esteban walked to Brody, put his arm around his shoulder and said, "Come with me, I'd like to have a little chat with you, my friend." They walked out of the back of the barn together.

"Now, tell me about you and my Rosie, will you?"

Brody didn't quite know what to say. "What did you want to know?" he finally asked.

"How long have you two had this relationship?" Esteban asked. "Don't kid me now. I saw you two together. I've seen that before. I see in you two how I feel about Cutter and how I think he feels about me."

Brody turned red in the face again and turned away from Esteban before he answered. "Rosie was my Bizzy Izzy. I was here when she was born. I got to know her then. She and I played together every day after school, and before school when I could sneak down to the barn. She and I became great friends. I was the first one to trail-ride her off the ranch. I helped teach her the reining patterns. We don't talk the same language, but we communicate. I know that's hard to believe since I'm a boy and she's a horse, but we can talk to each other. We understand each other. I've never had that feeling about a horse before. She is so special!"

"Son, you don't have to tell me about that. I have that kind of relationship with Cutter. I bought him as a weanling and spent time with him. I wanted the best for him. That's why I brought him to your Uncle Mike. We communicate too. It is different, but it is like being in love. That is something you will find out later. You have plenty of time for that."

"Then you don't think I'm crazy?" Brody asked him,

"No, not at all. I think you are a special person who has the capacity for loving and giving and that is not usual these days. I admire you for that."

"How long do I have before she leaves?" Brody asked bluntly. "How much time do I have with her?"

Esteban thought before he answered. "I need to run to the Hacienda Rancho for some things. I will be back with John and Rhonda, but it will be later this afternoon. Will that give you some time for her?"

Brody looked relieved but sad at the same time. "Yes, sir, that will give me time to say goodbye to her. I thank you very much." He turned away because his eyes were getting cloudy and he didn't want tears to show. He would be 15 years old, and 15-year-old boys never cried, especially in front of another man. Knowing Rosie was leaving again was like rubbing salt in that wound all over again. It hurt.

CHAPTER | THIRTY-FIVE

Rosie talked to her mother from their opposing stalls. *"Mom, I don't want to leave you, but I'd love to live here with Brody. How would you make it without me? Can you do that? I've been with you since the day I was born. If I were to stay here and you were to go home, I would miss you terribly. Would you miss me?"*

"My dear. You are probably getting the cart before the horse. John and Rhonda are coming to pick us up this afternoon. What makes you think you are going to stay here?"

"Mom, it's not what I think, it's what I wish! I would love to stay with Brody, but I would miss you more than I can tell you. I've been with you all my life. You've been my rock, my teacher, and my mother."

"Rosie, you don't need me any longer. You're grown up. You need to make a life of your own. If, and I quantify that as If, you stay here, I will not worry about you. Brody will be good for you as you will be good for him. You both need some time to grow up yet, but if you stay here, I'll not have to worry about you. Mike and Ginny are good people. You will have the best of care. I will not feel bad knowing you are somewhere with people who will be good to you. But I will miss you."

"But Mom, I will miss you so much," Rosie admitted tearfully.

"Yes, my child, I will miss you too, but it is the way of things. I know you will do great things. I know Brody will care for you. I know you will care for Brody. It is the best a mother can ask. But you may come home with me. If that is what happens, you will be taken care of either way, and I will get to see you every day. So, no matter what happens, I will be happy for you."

****

The four men made "bank" on the second day of the Rodeo. Each of them had ridden broncs or bulls, and each of them stayed on long enough for points that translated into dollars at the window. They took their tickets in and collected their winnings individually and added them up at the end of the night. They still had one more day of competition. They were ahead by over $400, not including what they'd spent on Friday night enjoying themselves. The people watching them gave them no clue they watched every move they made. They were oblivious to that. The reason they'd not been taken into custody before this was they were never together at the same time. There had been occasions when three of them were together, and two of them were together, but never all four of them at the same time until that Sunday morning. About 2:30 a.m. on Sunday, the last straggler of the bunch headed for the trailer a bit tipsy after leaving a young lady who ended up being uncooperative to his advances. He'd just opened the door to the trailer when deputies surrounded their trailer with badges and guns drawn.

Shocked beyond words, the four men stood outside the trailer allowing the deputies to handcuff them and stuff them into patrol cars for the ride to jail. Deputies shuffled each of them into separate interview rooms at the Yavapai County Sheriff's Office. Detectives or senior deputies interviewed them and quickly deduced that Merle was the brains of the group and he didn't have more than two brain cells to rub together to begin with.

"So what were you thinking, stealing a horse as high profile as Cut It Out anyway?" the senior detective asked Merle. "Did you actually think you could get away with this?"

Merle's feathers flipped. "Well, we didn't get no ransom so there's no harm and no foul is there?" he said with an attitude.

"No, you didn't collect a ransom on the horse because the owner was in Spain and never got your demand for two weeks. But you left that valuable horse out in the desert without food or water. What did you expect to happen to him? Did you realize he was worth $500,000 in today's money?" the detective asked him.

Merle was flustered but would not let on, "If you think I'd leave that much money on the table, you're crazy. We only asked for $100,000. If we'd thought he was worth a half a million, we'd have asked for that!"

"You disgust me. You chained two human beings to a cast iron headboard for days. What was your plan for them? They heard you talk about leaving them chained up and disappearing. What did you think would happen to them? Did you consider that you'd be charged with murder right now if they hadn't gotten free?"

"I ain't talking to you no more without my lawyer. Where's my lawyer? You have to provide us with a lawyer. I know our rights!" Merle shouted and shut down the conversation. He was the smart one of the bunch. The other three in separate interview rooms spilled their guts and told everything they knew.

CHAPTER | THIRTY-SIX

Esteban thought about Brody and Rosie. He thought about himself and Cutter. He knew what was the right thing to do. He owed Brody for the way he'd worked so hard to find his Cutter. He pulled Rosie's registration paperwork from the files at the Hacienda Rancho and rode with John and Rhonda back to Hartley Ranch with the horse trailer. He talked to his wife in Spain. After all that Brody did to help find Cutter, Rosie should belong to Brody. She agreed with him. It was the least they could do. They were going to bring five horses back to Hacienda Rancho, not six. Stevie decided at the last minute to come with them. He enjoyed Brody's company and wanted to see how he reacted to his father's idea.

They pulled in the driveway at Hartley Ranch. Mike waved them on to the barn so they could load their horses. Mike walked down with Ginny and Brody to the barn to help out.

They haltered the horses going home and walked them into the trailer one at a time.

Brody haltered Rosie himself and got in the back of the line in the barn with a sick feeling in the pit of his stomach. How would he see her again? It was painful when he found her gone the first time. How could he load her on the trailer to leave again? He swallowed hard and tried to keep his mind blank. He just didn't want to feel that pain of losing her once more and he didn't want to be the one who handed her off to someone else. His heart ached but he was determined it wouldn't show.

Rosie was heartbroken. Her Brody wouldn't even look at her. He was like a stone figure holding her lead rope. This was not the feeling she was used to getting from him. *"Mother, what is wrong? Why is he acting like this? I want to stay here with him and he won't even look at me right now? Have I done something wrong?"*

"No, my daughter. You have done nothing wrong. I don't think he wants you to go away again, but he is powerless to stop it. It is an odd thing with people. I remember the woman who owned my mother. She was very kind to me and I learned to respect her and look up to her. Then one day another woman came to see me. She was also kind to me. The two women talked to each other while I played with the other foals in the pasture. Then the other woman came with a trailer and brought me here. I missed my friends and my mother for a long time. After a while I met Luisa, Mr. Garcia's wife. I knew right away Luisa was my special person. I miss her right now and wish she was here. Miss Ginny taught me how to carry a rider, then taught Luisa how to ride on my back. She became my heart person. I love her dearly. But I had no control over where I was taken and by whom, and neither do you. But I know Mr. Garcia and John and Rhonda will take care of us."

"Mother, if I have to leave my Brody, it will break my heart again." Rosie whispered softly.

"You will miss him, I know. But your heart will not really break," her mother answered gently. *"You will miss him for while, but you must keep your mind open to possibilities."*

Esteban walked over to Brody and said, "She's not going anywhere. You can put her back in her stall."

Brody, confused, asked, "What do you mean?"

Esteban said, "Well, with your parent's permission, I would love to gift her to you. I can't thank you enough for all you did to help me find my Cutter. Please accept this gift of Desert Rose from me and my family."

Brody was not sure he heard what Mr. Garcia said, but Rosie did hear it and went a little nuts. She began squealing and whinnying and circling Brody on her lead rope as he stood confused and shook his head.

Desert Fire walked into the trailer with her head held high. She would miss her daughter dearly but she was happy for her at the same time. She was going to stay with her heart human. She wished she could spend time with Luisa. She would understand. Her own son, Stevie, was growing up and would soon leave. Mothers share that universally. They raise their children and watch them as they move away and form their own lives. *Have a good life, my daughter,* was all she could think.

"What I'm saying is that Rosie is your horse, now and forever. She loves you, and you love her. You two should be together. I have her registration paperwork here. I've signed it off to you, Brody, in thanks for helping to find my Cutter for me. Do you understand now?"

Ginny and Mike were standing looking at him as Rosie circled around him squealing and whinnying her head off. "Brody, you might want to calm your horse down a little so we can load the others," Uncle Mike said. "I think she needs some attention, don't you?"

The "your horse" finally sunk in. Brody was not sure how to act. His mind reeled with the realization that Rosie would never leave him again. He hugged his horse as if they were the only two creatures on the face of the planet. Then he hugged her some more for good measure struggling to keep his tears at bay. Rosie squealed her joy and hugged Brody back, pressing his body close to hers with her beautiful curved neck.

Thank you for joining Prince Ali and his friends, human, equine and all the furry beings that reside in their alternate world.

If you are enjoying our Wonder Horse series and have a moment, we would really appreciate a short review on the site where you bought this book. Your help in spreading the word about the series is invaluable and reviews make a big difference in helping new readers find the series.

https://www.wonderhorsebooks.com
https://www.Amazon.com
https://www.authormasterminds.com/victoria-hardesty-and-nancy-perez